Deception

CAROL OLIVER TURCOTTE

NEWMAN SPRINGS PUBLISHING
320 Broad Street
Red Bank, NJ 07701

First originally published by Newman Springs Publishing 2021

ISBN 978-1-63692-536-3 (Paperback)
ISBN 978-1-63692-537-0 (Digital)

Printed in the United States of America

To Melody, Mary, Diana, my mother, and
my husband, thank you for your encouragement.

Cast of Main Characters

Cassie Marshall—Journalist with the *St. Martin Herald*
Hawk Logan—Agent with the Drug Enforcement Agency
Steven Hollister—Lieutenant with the St. Martin's PD and close
    friend to Cassie Marshall
Trevor Marshall—Agent with the Federal Bureau of Investigation
    and brother to Cassie Marshall

Chapter 1

Cassie heard the anxious, fearful excitement in Carson's voice. "Carson, slow down. I don't understand what you're saying. What have you discovered?"

"Cassie, I don't have time to explain, but it involves Enrique Espinoza. I think I've finally got him!"

Cassandra Marshall couldn't believe what she was hearing. She and Carson Waynick had met in journalism class in college and had stayed in touch through the years. Recently, they had both set their sights on the same goal—proving that Enrique Espinoza was using his business as a front for his drug cartel. Cassie worked for the *St. Martin Herald and Carson* as a freelance writer. Neither of them, however, had succeeded in finding any solid evidence that would prove their suspicions.

"What do you mean? Carson, what do you have?" Cassie was excited but also concerned about the implications this could hold.

Carson sounded as though he was about to hyperventilate from the excitement enveloping him. "There's a huge deal going down tonight. It's going to be in Warehouse 3 at midnight. I'm going to position myself early and record the transaction. We'll finally have the proof we need to nail him."

"Carson, you can't be serious! Do you realize how dangerous that is? If you're caught, they'll kill you. Let me call Steven and have him bring a team to the warehouse."

Carson was livid. "No! I've worked too hard to get this, and I don't want the police ruining it. Meet me at the warehouse, Cassie. We'll both get an exclusive. This could be huge for your career too."

Cassie knew he was right, but she wasn't sure she was willing to take that kind of risk. She didn't want Carson to take that risk either. "Carson, please, don't do this. It's far too risky. Just—"

Carson cut her off. "I'm leaving now. If you want in on it, meet me there in thirty minutes. But don't call the cops."

"Carson—"

The line went dead. Cassie immediately punched in Steven's number. Steven Hollister was a lieutenant with the St. Martin police force. He and Cassie had been best friends since kindergarten.

"Hollister."

"Steven, it's Cassie. We've got a problem. Carson Waynick just called me and said there's a huge drug deal going down at midnight tonight in Warehouse 3. He said it's Espinoza."

"How did he get that information?"

"I don't know. He said he didn't have time to explain. But he's planning on recording the deal. Steven, I'm worried something is going to happen to him."

Steven knew Waynick and Cassie had both been chasing leads for over a year. He had also warned both of them to leave the detective work to the police, a warning neither had heeded, and now it could cost Waynick dearly.

"Cassie, you need to convince him to stay away. I'll get my team, and we'll take care of it."

"I tried. But he wouldn't listen. I'm going down there to try to stop him."

"No! Cassie, stay away from the waterfront. Let us take care of it."

"Steven, I can't let him walk into the middle of this deal. I have to try to stop him."

"Cassie—"

"Meet me at Warehouse 1. I'll wait for you to arrive. I promise. But I have to do something."

Steven had known Cassie long enough to know there would be no talking her out of going. "Fine. But don't go near Warehouse 3 until we arrive. Promise me, Cassie."

"I promise." She hung up and hurried for the door.

It was already almost ten. She had less than two hours to get Carson away from that warehouse. She tried texting Carson for what seemed like the hundredth time, but he was still not answering. She hated not being able to do anything on her own. But she promised Steven she would wait, so she would wait. Besides, she wasn't big on committing suicide, and walking into Warehouse 3 would most certainly be just that.

Steven Hollister and his team arrived at Warehouse 1 around eleven. He had called his friend Hawk Logan, who was an agent with the Drug Enforcement Agency, and he and his team had come along with him. Logan's team had been working the Espinoza case for over a year, and he hoped his team would be able to help.

They cautiously entered Warehouse 1, but there was no sign of Cassie or Carson.

Hawk looked at his friend. "So where are they? Do you think she went to Warehouse 3 without us?"

Steven shook his head. "No, she promised she would wait. Cassie is headstrong, but she would never break a promise. Something's not right. Let's head over to Warehouse 3."

Hawk wanted to believe Hollister, but he had a rather negative attitude toward journalists, especially journalists who thought they could break a huge story. As they silently rounded the corner and made their way toward Warehouse 3, they were suddenly met with a barrage of gunfire.

Chapter 2

Hawk Logan instantly took charge. "Take cover!"

Both teams quickly ran to get something between them and the gunfire. Bullets were flying from the upper windows of Warehouse 3. Steven and Hawk's teams both began to return fire. It was impossible to tell just how many assailants were firing on them. After about fifteen minutes of constant battling, the gunfire from the warehouse stopped.

Hawk yelled to the men, "Hold your fire!"

Steven had made his way behind the dumpster where Hawk had taken cover. He looked at Hawk and asked, "What are you thinking?"

Hawk never took his eyes off of the warehouse as he answered, "Other than the fact that they knew we were coming?"

"You think we were set up?"

He turned his face toward Steven. "How else would they have known we were coming?"

Steven had known Hawk a long time. He heard the contempt in his voice and knew exactly what he was thinking.

"Carson is a jerk, but I really don't think he would set us up. And it definitely wasn't Cassie. But we need to find her."

Hawk made no other comments on the subject. "I have two men down. How about you?"

"One. I've called for backup and EMTs. We need to get inside. I have a bad feeling that Cassie and Waynick may be in that warehouse."

"Pretty sure the assailants are gone, but we still need to be extra cautious."

Not something Steven needed to be told, but he said nothing. He continued to let Hawk take the lead. They had a total of twelve officers with them, and three of them were down.

"Jenkins, you and Thomas stay with the wounded men. Everyone else, with us. We're looking for Cassandra Marshall and Carson Waynick. Hollister has a picture of Ms. Marshall which he is sending to your phones. We don't have a picture of Waynick, but if they are inside, chances are they are together. Let's proceed with caution."

The seven officers cautiously made their way to the front of the warehouse, using as much cover as possible. There was no more gunfire from the warehouse. Slowly, carefully, Hawk opened the front door as Steven and two other officers covered him. They entered the warehouse without incident and scanned the room.

After a few seconds, Steven broke the silence. "Do you smell smoke?"

Hawk had also noticed the smell of smoke as soon as they opened the door. "Yes. They may have set a fire before making their escape. We need to hurry."

He motioned for three of the officers to go to the left and three to go to the right; and he, Steven, and the remaining officer moved toward the back of the warehouse.

"Fifteen minutes. No more. We don't need to get trapped in the fire. This is an old warehouse, and it will go up fast. Move out."

As Steven and Hawk made their way to the back, they passed the lifeless bodies of three assailants. The room was quickly beginning to fill with smoke, and they could see flames coming from the back of the warehouse.

Steven nodded toward the back room. "My guess is, if Cassie and Waynick are in here, they're in that room."

Hawk agreed. "That would be my guess too. Let's check it out."

They quickly and cautiously made their way to the office at the back of the warehouse where the flames were rapidly beginning to grow. The door was jammed, and they couldn't get it opened. While the other officer covered them, Steven and Hawk kicked the door until it finally broke open. Carson Waynick was lying by a desk in a puddle of blood. Steven checked for a pulse but couldn't find one.

"Steven! Over here!"

Steven hurried to the other side of the room where he found Hawk with Cassandra. He had lifted her into his arms by the time Steven arrived.

"Is she alive?"

"She has a pulse, but she has a head wound and appears to have been shot. We need to get her out of here. What about Waynick?"

Steven shook his head. "He's dead."

"Let's go. I've got her. Radio the men and get everyone out of here. That fire is spreading fast."

They exited the building just as the first responders arrived. Steven's officer was dead, and one of the DEA agents was critical. They loaded all the injured, including Cassie, into ambulances; and Steven and Hawk followed behind them to the hospital.

For several minutes, Steven and Hawk rode in silence. Steven was very aware of Hawk's feelings toward journalists, and he had no doubt of his opinion of Cassie even though he knew nothing about her.

Steven eventually broke the silence by saying, "I don't care what you think right now. I know Cassie had nothing to do with any of this. But regardless of how you feel, I know you're a Christian. Do me a favor and lift a prayer for Cassie."

Hawk never took his eyes off the road as he answered, "I already have."

Chapter 3

Cassie was rushed to an exam room in the ER at St. Martin Medical Center. Steven and Hawk waited anxiously in the hall outside the exam room. The silence between them was palpable. The two men had been friends for a long time, but the doubts and tension were quickly creating a wall they needed to tear down.

As they leaned against the hospital wall, Steven finally spoke, "Hawk, I just ask that you withhold judgment until we talk to Cassie. I know this looks bad, but I've known Cassie almost my entire life. She's a strong Christian and would never do anything immoral or illegal. I also know you have a strong distrust of journalists, which I totally understand, but Cassie isn't like most journalists. Just give her a chance to explain."

Hawk didn't answer immediately, which had Steven concerned that he wouldn't be open minded about this situation.

Finally, he answered, "We've been friends for a long time, Hollister, and if you say I can trust her... I'll trust her. But I want to hear what she has to say. There are a lot of unanswered questions."

Steven slowly nodded his head without looking at Hawk. "I agree. Thanks, Logan."

"Don't thank me yet. We haven't heard what she has to say."

That concerned Steven too.

An hour later, the doctor came out of the ER room and found Steven and Hawk waiting outside the door. "Officers, I'm Dr. Howard. Ms. Marshall is quite fortunate. She was apparently hit over the head with a blunt object, causing a large gash and the blood on her head. The injury required eight stitches, and she has a concussion and will have quite a headache for a while."

Steven asked, "What about the gunshot wound?"

"Again, a fortunate young lady. The bullet grazed her upper arm. It was a deep injury requiring stitches, but just skin damage. No muscles or bones were injured. Her arm is going to be sore for several days, and she needs to wear a sling for about a week and avoid using the arm as much as possible. Overall, she's going to be fine. We'll be sending her up to a room in a bit. I want her to spend the night here so we can monitor the head wound. If all goes well, she can go home in twenty-four hours."

Steven shook Dr. Howard's hand. "Thank you, Doctor. Can we go in and see her?"

"Sure. Just don't overdo the visit. I gave her some mild pain medication, but she is still going to be hurting and exhausted."

"Understood."

Dr. Howard left them as they turned to go into Cassie's room. Steven walked over to the bed and lifted another prayer of thanks that she was alive and well.

He smiled as she turned her head on the pillow to look at him, and he softly spoke to her, "Hi, honey. You gave us quite a scare."

Quietly, Cassie responded, "Hi, yourself. I kind of gave myself a scare." Tears began to roll down her face. "I'm so sorry, Steven. I didn't know. I tried to wait, but they knew I was there. I'm so sorry."

Gently, Steven stroked her hair. "It's okay, Cas. You're okay. We'll talk later. Right now, you need to rest."

Cassie slowly nodded her head as her eyes landed on Hawk. He had been quietly standing by the door, allowing Steven this time with his friend and silently watching her response.

Steven noticed her looking at Hawk, whom he had momentarily forgotten about. "Cas, this is my friend Hawk Logan. He's the one who actually found you and carried you out of the warehouse."

Cassie smiled a timidly weak smile. "Thank you."

Hawk couldn't explain the feeling that suddenly overtook him. It was a feeling of protectiveness and...so much more. There was something in those soft brown eyes that bore a hole into his heart.

With an unusually soft voice, he answered, "You're welcome."

The nurse came in to get Cassie ready to move to a room.

Steven leaned over and gently kissed her cheek. "We'll see you in a while after they get you moved to a room."

Cassie grabbed his hand with a look of fear in her eyes. "You're not leaving?"

The sudden fear in Cassie did not go unnoticed by Steven or Hawk.

Softly, he answered, "No, honey, we're not leaving. We have some business to take care of, but we're not leaving the hospital. We'll be up once you're settled in your room."

She seemed to calm some at that reply and relaxed against the pillow. Steven and Hawk left the room.

Once they were in the hall, Hawk turned to Steven. "There's something else going on here. I don't even know her, but I could tell she was terrified."

"Yeah, I know. That's not like Cassie at all. Once she's settled and rested some, we'll find out what she knows."

Once Cassie was settled in her room, she quickly fell asleep and slept for the next four hours. Steven and Hawk stood in the hall outside her room, ready to go in and ask her some questions.

"Hawk, I think it might be best if you question Cassie. I think she might open up more to someone she doesn't know. She might be afraid to tell me everything. Besides, this is going to be a DEA case, not an SMPD case, so all the more reason for you to do the questioning."

"That might be a good idea. But if you think you might get more information at any point, feel free to jump in."

"Deal." Steven opened the door, and they walked into Cassie's hospital room.

Cassie turned her head toward the door and smiled as she saw Steven come into the room. She also felt her heart beat a little faster as she watched Hawk come in behind Steven. She wasn't sure what the feelings were she was having, but something inside her stirred when she looked at Hawk Logan.

Steven tenderly kissed her cheek and sat in the chair beside her bed. "You look a little more rested. How are you feeling?"

"I've definitely felt better, but I'm okay."

Hawk pulled up a chair on the other side of the bed. "We're definitely glad you're doing better. Do you feel up to answering some questions?"

"I'll try."

"Can you just start from the phone call with Steven? What happened after you got to the warehouse district?"

Cassie took a deep breath and closed her eyes. Steven reached over and took her hand in his.

He softly said, "Take your time. Just tell us whatever you remember. You can stop if it gets too hard."

She squeezed his hand then started to relate all she could recall. "I arrived at Warehouse 1 around ten thirty. I sat in my car for a while, texting Carson, but he wasn't answering. It was eerily quiet on the waterfront, which was a bit disconcerting, but I went inside to see if I could find Carson. It was dark inside, and I didn't see anyone for several minutes. Finally, I saw Carson come in a side door. But he wasn't alone. There were two men with him."

Hawk asked, "Did you recognize the men who were with Carson?"

Cassie nodded her head. "One of them was one of the security guards at Espy Enterprises."

Hawk and Steven exchanged concerned glances.

"Are you sure?"

"Positive. I remember him because he always creeped me out when I saw him."

"What happened after Carson came in with the two men?"

"That's where it gets sketchy. I asked Carson what was going on, but before I got an answer, someone hit me over the head, and everything went black. The next thing I remember, I woke up in an office. I assumed it was in Warehouse 3, but I didn't really know. Carson was arguing with someone, so I stayed still and tried to hear what they were saying." She stopped as a sob caught in her chest and tears welled in her eyes.

Hawk's heart went out to this beautiful lady. He reached over and put his hand tenderly on her arm.

Tears rolled down her face as he gently spoke, "It's okay, Cassie. It can't hurt you now. Steven and I aren't going to let anything happen to you."

In that moment, Hawk knew those weren't just words. He would do whatever necessary to protect her.

Cassie knew nothing about Hawk Logan, but she completely trusted that he meant exactly what he was saying. She looked into his steel-blue eyes and felt safe and protected.

She nodded her head and took a deep breath as she responded, "Carson set me up. He set us all up."

Steven couldn't believe what he was hearing. "What do you mean, Cas? What did you hear them saying?"

"Carson was yelling at them. He was saying that I wasn't supposed to be hurt. That wasn't part of the deal. I couldn't hear what the other man was saying. I couldn't get a good look at the third man, but I'm almost certain it was Espinoza. But like I said, I never got a clear look at him."

"How did you get shot?"

"I heard them talking about the police coming and that they were ready for them. They wouldn't know what hit them." She stopped and looked at Steven as she squeezed his hand, tears rolling down her face. "They were going to kill you. I had to warn you. They had taken my cell, but there was a phone on the desk in the office. I didn't even know if it worked or not, but I had to try. So while they were arguing, I carefully pulled myself up to the desk and made my way over to the phone. My head was pounding, and it was all I could do to not pass out, but I managed somehow. I had just picked up the receiver and punched in a couple of numbers when the door burst open. Everything happened so fast. The man was pointing a gun at me and yelling in Spanish. Carson rushed in and jumped in front of me. He yelled, 'No!' just as the gun went off." She took a deep breath and quietly asked, "Carson's dead, isn't he?"

Steven answered, "Yes, honey. We found him on the floor of the office with a through-and-through gunshot wound to the chest. Is that when you got shot?"

"Yes. I think so. I fell to the floor and felt the room spinning. The man was aiming the gun at me, but I heard someone yell that they were here, so he locked the door and left. The last thing I remember is lifting a prayer of protection for you and all the responding officers. Was anyone hurt?"

"One officer was killed, and a couple of DEA agents were wounded."

"I'm so sorry." Tears continued to pour down her face. "I had no idea it was a setup. I can't believe Carson was in on this. Why would he do this to me, Steven? He was my friend."

"I don't know what happened, Cas, but my guess would be money. Hopefully, we'll know more once we go through his apartment."

Hawk knew she was spent and she needed to rest. They had all the information she had anyway.

He rubbed her arm as he spoke, "Cassie, you did great. Don't worry about any of this. Leave this to us. We'll figure out what's going on. We're going to go and let you get some rest."

He pulled his hand away from her arm, and Cassie instantly felt an emptiness and a little less secure.

"Thank you, Hawk. I'm really glad I've had a chance to meet you. I just wish it had been under better circumstances."

Hawk smiled warmly at Cassie. "Me too. Get some rest. We'll be back later." He stood up and headed toward the door.

Steven stood and tenderly kissed his friend's cheek. "I love you, Cassie. Just so you know, there will be a guard outside your door tonight. We don't think you're still in danger, but since we aren't sure what we're dealing with yet, we don't want to take any chances. We'll be back first thing in the morning. Rest well, hon."

"Thank you, Steven. I'm really glad you're okay. I love you too."

He smiled as he squeezed her hand and then walked to the door with Hawk.

Hawk looked at his friend. "So what's bothering you?"

Steven smiled. "That obvious, huh?"

"Probably just to me. But I've known you a long time, and I can tell when you're not being completely honest."

Steven became very serious as he answered, "What I just told Cassie wasn't the truth. And if she wasn't feeling so lousy, she would have known I was lying too. You and I both know that, if the Espinoza Cartel is behind this, they're not going to stop until Cassie is dead. They obviously left her for dead in that warehouse, but she didn't die, so she's still a threat."

Hawk didn't like what he was hearing, mainly because it just confirmed what he had already been thinking. "I know you're right, but there's not much we can do for now. Everyone is looking for Espinoza, but he's gone dark. He's totally off the radar."

"Well, I'm not going to let him get to Cassie. We need to find something on him, and we need to find it fast."

"DEA is working on processing everything we found in Waynick's apartment, but nothing implicating Espinoza yet. They're going by Cassie's house tomorrow before she goes home."

Steven narrowed his eyes. "Why are they going to Cassie's? She's not a suspect."

Hawk understood Steven's concern. "No, she's not a suspect, but she is a target. We're actually sweeping for bugs and possible explosives."

"So you think she's still in danger too."

"It's a strong possibility. Since this is our case, I feel we need to do our best to protect her."

Steven slowly nodded his head. "Let's go get some rest. Tomorrow is going to be a long day."

The two men left the hospital and headed home.

Cassie had been trying to sleep for a while, but she couldn't calm her mind enough to actually sleep. She knew it was probably time for the nurse to come back in and check on her, so she closed her eyes and tried to rest a while longer until the nurse came in. When she heard the door open, she knew her rest was over for now. But for some unexplainable reason, she had a very uneasy feeling. She opened her eyes and slowly turned toward the door. Just as she turned onto her back, she saw the pillow coming down to cover her face.

Chapter 4

S teven had been home for about three hours but simply couldn't sleep. He got dressed and decided to go back to the hospital and sit with Cassie. Maybe he could catch a little sleep there. He just felt uneasy leaving her in that hospital bed alone. Even though there was a guard on the door, he couldn't shake the feeling of dread that drenched him. He grabbed his keys and headed out the door.

Cassie gasped for air as the pillow blocked her airways.

Lord, please help me. Show me what to do.

She knew she needed to get the guard's attention, but how? She needed to make some noise, but she couldn't scream. She could barely breathe. The IV. Maybe she could pull the IV stand over and make enough noise to get the guard's attention. She reached her hand out and grabbed hold of the IV tubing. She was fighting to remain conscious.

Lord, give me strength.

She pulled the tube with all the strength she had left. The IV stand came crashing to the floor, hitting the side table in the process. The IV jerked out of her arm, and the tubing wrapped around the cords attached to the monitor, pulling them loose. There was a loud crash, and all the monitor signals started going off. But Cassie didn't hear any of it. She had lost consciousness.

Steven had stopped at the vending machine to get some coffee for himself and the officer on guard duty outside Cassie's room.

"Hey, Lieutenant. I thought you went home to get some rest."

Steven smiled. "I thought I did too. Couldn't sleep, so decided to just come back and sit with Cassie. How's everything been around here?"

"Pretty quiet. The nurse is in with her now."

The sound of something falling and crashing on the floor came from inside Cassie's room. At the same instant, the monitor alarms started sounding. Without hesitation, Steven and the officer dropped their coffee and burst into Cassie's room, guns drawn.

Steven saw the man standing over Cassie with the pillow in his hands, and his heart felt like it jumped up into his throat.

He aimed his gun at the man. "Step away from the bed! Now!"

The man stood still for a few seconds and then slowly started to straighten up.

"Put your hands up!"

The man started to raise one hand and began to turn. Suddenly there was a large pop and the sound of glass breaking. The man jerked and fell to the ground in a pool of blood. Steven and the other officer quickly moved away from the window as Steven made his way to Cassie's bed. She wasn't breathing, and there was no pulse. Without hesitation, he began CPR.

Several nurses had made their way to the room and now rushed to assist. The man on the floor was dead, and nothing could be done for him. So they all turned their attention on Cassie. After a few minutes of CPR, she had a pulse and was breathing again. One of the nurses hooked up some oxygen while another nurse bandaged her arm where the IV was yanked out when she pushed over the IV stand.

Once Steven knew she was okay, he had her moved to another room, and this room was taped off as it was now a crime scene. As soon as she was settled in a new room, he called Hawk.

An obviously half-asleep Hawk answered the phone. "Hollister, do you have any idea what time it is?"

"I do. And we have a problem."

Hawk was instantly awake, his thoughts unexplainably on Cassie. "What kind of problem?"

"Someone just tried to kill Cassie."

"What! In the hospital room? Is she okay?"

"Thankfully, she will be fine. But this situation just got a lot more complicated."

With a sound of urgency in his voice, Hawk replied, "I'll be there in fifteen."

Chapter 5

Hawk stood outside Cassie's room listening in disbelief to what Steven was telling him. "So do we know who this man was? Was he one of Espinoza's men?"

"Not exactly. He had worked here at the medical center for over two years as an LPN. My guess is Espinoza gave him an irresistible offer and hired him to kill Cassie. He wasn't even a plant. Obviously, we can't trust anyone. He was able to get past the guard because he had been cleared."

"So we really have no choice. We need to get Cassie to a safe house, now."

"My thoughts exactly. I'm not sure if Espinoza thinks she can ID him from the warehouse or if he thinks she has some kind of information, but he's obviously bent on eliminating Cassie. We have to get her to a safe place. Fast."

Hawk had a look of determination on his face. "I've got this. We have a safe house that's available, and I can get her there tonight. Will she be able to travel?"

"I think so. This incident may have set her back some, but I know she's ready to get out of here. She's really stressing out."

"I can understand that. But if we don't nail Espinoza soon, this could get a lot worse."

Steven knew Hawk was right, but hearing it said out loud made it all too real. "Is your team getting close?"

"We are, but nothing we can make stick. We have to find that one nail that's going to put this case down."

"We'll find it. We have to."

Hawk was concerned about Cassie's safety. Espinoza was a ruthless drug lord. The fact that they had not yet found that one piece of the puzzle to put him away for good didn't change the facts. He would kill his own mother if she got in his way. He had already made two attempts on Cassie's life. Hawk knew he wasn't going to give up.

"I'll get us a couple of burner phones so we can communicate. We can't take a chance of him tracing our cells. I'll switch out vehicles in case there's been a tracking device put on mine."

Steven nodded his head in agreement. "Sounds good. Why don't you go in and stay with Cassie while I wrap up the shooting with my captain. I don't want to leave her alone even with a guard on the door."

"Sure. I'll go let her know what's happening."

Hawk didn't really know Cassie, but he was about to get to know her a lot better. They were going to be spending a lot of time together, and he wasn't really sure how he was feeling about that.

Lord, I can't explain what I feel when I'm around Cassie, but I know I have to keep her safe. Please help me focus on the job at hand and not the feelings that are growing within me.

He took a deep breath and opened the door.

Cassie sat on the side of her hospital bed, wiping the tears from her eyes. She had never prayed so much in her life. In less than twenty-four hours, there had been two attempts on her life, and three people were dead. She knew Enrique Espinoza was a dangerous man, but what had she gotten herself into? Her thoughts drifted to Hawk Logan. What was it about this man? Had God placed him here to help her through this situation? She couldn't explain it, but there was a sense of peace and safety when he was around. As she wiped more tears, she turned with a start when she heard the door open. She felt her breath catch when she saw Hawk standing in the doorway.

Hawk saw the tears and wanted to pull her into his arms and tell her everything was going to be okay. Instead, he pulled out a tissue from the box on the side table and handed it to her as he sat down in the chair across from her.

"Cassie, I'm sorry you're having to go through this. I know it's hard, but we're closing in on Espinoza. We're going to make sure he can't get to you."

"Yeah, that hasn't been working so well."

"No, it hasn't. But I'm taking you to a safe house tonight."

Cassie wasn't expecting that. "You're…what? A safe house? Are you serious?" Fresh tears formed in her eyes.

Hawk couldn't resist any longer. He stood and walked to the bed where he sat down and pulled Cassie into his arms. She laid her head on his chest and let the tears flow.

"Cassie, I know this is hard, but we're going to get through this…together. I promise I'm not going to let anything happen to you."

Cassie sniffed and wiped her eyes. She raised her head and looked into Hawks steel-blue eyes. They were full of compassion and strength, and she knew she was safe with him. But even he couldn't guarantee what he was promising.

"You know you can't promise that. I mean, I believe you will do everything in your power to protect me…but this is Enrique Espinoza. He's a very dangerous man."

Hawk knew she was right. "I may not be able to promise it with a 100 percent guarantee, but you can believe I will do everything in my power to keep you safe."

A slight smiled crossed Cassie's face. "I do believe that."

She dried her face and set up as she moved from the security of Hawk's arms. Although she would have been happy to have stayed there all night, she knew it wasn't really appropriate. He was basically her bodyguard, not her love interest.

"But why is he after me? I don't know anything."

"Our best guess is that Waynick set you up to get the heat off of himself. Did he really have information that could nail Espinoza?"

"I don't know. It's definitely possible. I hadn't talked to Carson in months until he called me yesterday. I know he had done some pretty deep digging, but I don't know if he had found anything. We didn't really share our findings with each other. I wish I knew something. At least then, this would at least make sense."

Hawk could tell Cassie was getting tired. They would be leaving in a couple of hours, and she probably needed to get some rest before they started their trip. They would be in the car for almost two hours.

"Even if you did know something, none of this would make sense." He gently placed his hand on top of her hand. "We'll be leaving soon. Why don't you try to get some rest? I'll be right outside the door. And no one is coming into this room unless I come with them."

Cassie's heart beat a little faster at the touch of Hawk's hand on hers. "Thank you, Hawk. I appreciate all you're doing for me."

Hawk smiled and then reluctantly stood and left the room as Cassie laid back down on the bed and pulled the blanket up. Her head was pounding, and her arm was throbbing. She knew she needed some rest—she just wasn't sure she could.

Steven had gone by Cassie's house to get her some clothes and personal items to take with her to the safe house. It had taken him longer than he planned because, when he opened her front door, he saw that her house had been ransacked. He had to wait for the forensic team to come dust for prints before he could get what he needed. He wouldn't tell Cassie about her house—at least, not yet. She didn't need that extra stress added to her plate right now. Once it was fully processed, he would go back and try to get it straightened up some before Cassie came home. Hopefully, that would be soon.

He walked into Cassie's room and found her dressed and sitting on the side of the bed. Hawk was standing on the far side of the room, talking to someone on his phone. He acknowledged Steven as he walked in and indicated he would be right with him. Steven walked over to Cassie and pulled her into a hug as he kissed her cheek.

"How are you holding up?"

"I'm okay."

Steven smiled at his friend. "Liar."

Cassie gave a small laugh. "Well, I'm okay…considering."

Steven sat down beside her and held her hand. "Honey, it's going to be okay. Hawk is the best. You couldn't be in better hands. He'll keep you safe." *Or die trying.* But he wasn't about to say that out loud. *Please, Lord, put a hedge of protection around Cassie and Hawk. Shield them from the evil that is Enrique Espinoza.*

Hawk ended his call and joined Steven and Cassie. He handed Steven a burner phone. "We got you this phone. It is untraceable, so we should be able to stay in contact without Espinoza finding out where the safe house is located. My team is still following leads, and we think we are closing in on Espinoza. I've switched vehicles, and we're going to take a lot of detours on the way to the house. I'll call you as soon as we get there."

"Hawk, thanks for doing this. I know you don't have to. We're going to keep working our leads also. We'll stay in contact with your team, and maybe between both agencies working this, we'll get something."

"We'll get what we need." He turned toward Cassie. "Are you ready?"

"As ready as I can be."

Steven helped her stand from the bed.

She wrapped her good arm around his neck and kissed his cheek. "Thank you for everything. Be safe. I couldn't bear it if anything happened to you."

"Don't worry about me. I'll be fine." He looked at Hawk. "Take care of her."

"I will guard her with my life."

Cassie didn't like the sound of that. She prayed no more lives would be lost in all this madness. *Keep us safe, Lord.*

Chapter 6

They arrived at the safe house about two hours later. Cassie looked at the pretty oceanfront, three-story home. Hawk came around and helped her out of his truck.

"This is a beautiful home. But it's not a safe house, is it? This is your home."

Hawk smiled. "What makes you say that?"

"Well, for one, it doesn't look like a safe house. It's too open. Also, you were far too familiar with the backroads and detours. It was like you were driving somewhere you had driven to a thousand times.

Hawk was in awe of this woman. "You're good." He smiled. "Steven and I decided all our safe houses might be compromised since we don't know who we can trust, so we said that's where we were going but decided to come here instead. Steven and I are the only people who know where we are. This isn't going to be at the top of Espinoza's list of locations, so it should buy us some time. Let's get you inside. You're hurting, aren't you?"

"A little." Actually, a lot, but she didn't want to concern him. "Riding in a vehicle probably wouldn't be top on my list right now."

Hawk came around and helped Cassie out of the truck and up the stairs of the beach home. "Let's get you settled inside, and I'll come back and get your bags."

He opened the door, and Cassie caught her breath as she looked around the spacious home.

"This is gorgeous. Is this really where you live?"

"It really is. I found it a couple of years ago, and it was perfect for me. It's spacious, secluded, and right on the beach. But it does get rather lonely sometimes."

"I know what you mean."

"Would you like to go sit in the sunroom? There's a comfortable recliner, and you can look out at the ocean."

"That sounds nice."

The view from the windows was absolutely breathtaking. Hawk had his own private lakefront beach. The sun would soon be setting, and the sky was a soothing shade of orange and yellow. Hawk helped her get settled into the recliner. He picked up a pillow from the couch and placed it under her arm and then covered her with an afghan from the end of the couch.

"Oh, that feels good. Thank you, Hawk."

"You're welcome. I'll get you some ibuprofen since I'm sure you are needing some. Would you like some water, cola, tea?"

"Just some water. Thanks."

Hawk brought her a couple of ibuprofen and a glass of water. "I'll go get your bags out of the truck and put them in your room. I'll be right back. Do you need anything else?"

"No, I'm good."

Hawk brought Cassie's bags inside and put them in the bedroom across the hall from his. He checked all the windows and doors to be sure they were secure and then went back to the sunroom where he found Cassie asleep. He watched her as she slept and was overcome with a feeling of—what? It felt like he was falling in love with her, but how could that be possible? He had only met her a couple of days earlier, and he barely knew her. It was probably just that sense of protectiveness. That had to be it. This was just a job. He couldn't risk getting personally involved. He pulled the afghan up around Cassie's shoulders, resisting the urge to kiss her forehead, and then turned and left the room.

He fixed himself a cup of coffee and then went to his office to call Steven. "Hey, man. Is there any more news?"

"Not really. They finished processing Waynick's apartment and found nothing of any use. Of course, they're still working on his laptop and tablet, but so far, there's been nothing there. If he has something on Espinoza, I don't think it's on his devices or in any of his files. How's Cassie?"

"Wiped out. She's sleeping right now."

"Has she remembered anything yet?"

"No. But she's still in a lot of pain and trying to process everything. I'll talk with her later and see if, possibly, she might recall something. Let me know if you hear anything."

"I will. Watch your back, Hawk. We both know how dangerous and resourceful Espinoza is."

"Yes, I know. You be careful too, Steven. He's going to be watching you."

"I know. I'll be in touch tomorrow."

Hawk hung up and pulled out the folder on Espinoza, hoping he would see something that he hadn't seen the first hundred times he had gone through the case file. He had been on this case for a year and a half. They were getting so close to nailing him. They just needed that one thing that would be the icing on the cake and put him away for good. Maybe Cassie held the missing piece. They would talk later when she was feeling better.

Cassie woke with a start and a tremendous headache. She sat up in bed, trying to orient herself to her surroundings. Reality slowly sank into her head. She was in Hawk Logan's house, trying to hide from Enrique Espinoza. She looked around the bedroom and vaguely remembered coming in here the night before. She had slept for a while in the recliner, then woke up, and ate a little; then Hawk showed her to her bedroom.

Hawk Logan. Just thinking about him made her head hurt even more. When he was near, she felt safe and protected. She also felt a lot more. He was tall, strong, gorgeous, and compassionate. Definitely someone she could see herself falling for. But he was here to protect her, not to love her. She knew he was just doing a job. He had no personal interest in her, so she needed to keep her feelings strictly business.

Cassie slowly got out of bed and went to the bathroom and splashed some water on her face. Maybe not the best idea. Her head throbbed even more as the cold water hit her face. She stepped into the hall and made her way toward the kitchen where she could smell bacon and…pancakes?

Hawk turned as Cassie entered the kitchen. The desire to pull her into his arms was overwhelming.

With a smile, he pushed those thoughts to the back of his mind. "Good morning. No offense, but you don't look so great. Is your head hurting?"

Cassie managed a slight smile. "No offense taken. And yes, my head is pounding. Would you happen to have some ibuprofen to go with that bacon?"

Hawk reached for the bottle of pills and a glass of orange juice. "I do. Maybe this will kick in pretty fast."

"I sure hope so. Do I smell pancakes?"

"You do. I hope you like chocolate chip pancakes."

"Oh, wow. Are you serious? That's my favorite."

"Good. Mine too. Why don't you go relax in the sunroom and let those ibuprofen take effect while I finish up? I'll bring it out when it's done. Would you like some coffee?"

"Actually, I think maybe just some more of this orange juice. I'm not sure I want coffee with my head hurting so much."

"Okay. Go rest, and I'll be out there in a few minutes."

Hawk watched her go to the sunroom and felt his breath catch as he watched her. *Lord, please help me protect her. I can't let anything happen to her.*

The next few days went by without incident. They talked to Steven every day, and there was still no sign of Espinoza. Cassie was feeling better every day. She was no longer wearing her sling and was only taking ibuprofen for the pain maybe once a day rather than every few hours. She was finally beginning to feel like herself again, so Hawk knew it was time to try to push her memory and see if maybe she could recall anything that might help them end this nightmare.

They had finished their dinner and were relaxing in the den. "So, Cassie, do you feel up to talking?"

Cassie smiled. "I thought we had been talking."

Hawk laughed. "Well, now that you're feeling better, I was thinking maybe we could dig a little deeper into your memory. See if we could trigger something."

"Yeah, I figured that was what you meant. I've been racking my brain the last few days, but I really can't think of anything useful."

"Let's think back to that last day you saw Carson, when you dropped in on him unexpectedly. Did you notice anything out of place? Did Carson do or say anything that struck you as odd? Anything you can remember could be helpful even if it seems like nothing."

"I don't know. I mean, he did seem a little stressed, but I'm not sure why."

"Go back to the beginning. Walk me through your visit from the moment he opened the door."

"Okay, I'll do my best to remember. It's been several months. Like I said, he seemed a little stressed when he let me in. I didn't know if it was because of me or something he had been working on when I arrived."

There was something to draw on.

"So he was working on something when you arrived? Do you know what it was?"

Cassie shook her head. "No. He didn't say. Actually, before we sat down to talk, he went to his desk and closed his laptop." Cassie gasped as a memory flashed into her head.

Hawk gently put his hand on her leg. "What is it, Cassie? Did you remember something?"

"I can't believe I didn't remember this sooner. When he closed his laptop, he pulled out a flash drive and tossed it in the desk drawer. He tried to do it subtly, like he didn't want me to know what he was doing. He seemed nervous while we were talking, and he kept glancing at his desk. He almost seemed relieved when I stood to leave. Maybe that flash drive is the missing puzzle piece."

Hawk didn't want to get overly excited, but he was definitely hopeful. "It's possible. Do you have any idea what he did with the drive?"

"No. Like I said, that was the last time I talked to him until he called me wanting me to meet him at the warehouse." She looked at Hawk, knowing he wasn't going to like what she was about to say. "We need to go to Carson's apartment."

Hawk was instantly shaking his head. "No. It's way too risky. Espinoza probably has men watching the building."

"I know. But the agents didn't find any flash drives, and we can assume Espinoza's men didn't either, or they wouldn't still be after me. I knew Carson. I know how his brain worked. I might be able to figure out where he put it. If he hid it in the apartment, I could possibly locate it. This could be exactly what we need to get Espinoza."

"You're probably right, but I don't like it. I'll go and see if I can find it."

"No. I have to go. Like I said, I know how Carson thinks...or thought. I might know where to look. Besides, two of us would be faster than one. Also, are you really going to go off and leave me here unprotected?"

Hawk shook his head as he smiled. "There's just no winning with you, is there?"

"You get to spend more time with me. Isn't that winning?"

Definitely. Hawk relented. "Okay. We'll go first thing in the morning. But I'm calling Steven. At least, we can have him and his men covering the building."

"Hawk, I know this is risky. But we can't just continue to sit around and do nothing. We need to be proactive here. We'll be careful and get in and out as quickly as possible."

Hawk didn't like it, but he knew she was right. It was a risk they had to take. He called Steven and coordinated with him. They would go to the apartment building at three o'clock tomorrow morning. Going early would give them a better chance of getting in undetected, and there would also be fewer people out and about that early in the morning—just in case things didn't go well.

Lord, I don't have a good feeling about this, yet I know it's the right move. Please protect Cassie and me. Help us find that flash drive and get out of there safely. Protect Steven and his team also. I'm worried about what we could be walking into tomorrow.

Chapter 7

The streets were eerily quiet in the early morning darkness as Hawk and Cassie pulled up behind Carson's apartment building.

He reached over and squeezed Cassie's hand. "Are you sure you're okay with this? We can back out. It's not too late."

Cassie gave him a weak smile. "No, I'm okay. I won't lie. I'm a little nervous, but I know we have to do this. Go ahead and call Steven."

Hawk gave her hand another squeeze before letting go of it. He pulled out his phone and punched in Steven's number. He answered before it even finished ringing.

"We're behind the building. Are your men in place?"

"We're all in position. Keep your phone on speaker, and I will too. It's not as good as having our earpieces, but it's better than nothing."

"I will. We're going in. We'll go as fast as possible."

"Hawk, I know I don't have to tell you this, but be careful. We have eyes on every side of the building, but that's still no guarantee—especially when we're dealing with Enrique Espinoza."

"I know. We'll be careful. You do the same."

Hawk got out of his truck and had Cassie slide over and exit on the driver side so she would be more shielded. He checked his surroundings, and then they entered the building and made their way up the stairs to Carson Waynick's third-floor apartment. They cautiously walked down the hall, and Hawk quickly opened the door to the apartment.

"Okay, Cassie, what are you thinking?"

Cassie was looking around the apartment, taking in all the nooks and crannies. "Carson was really intrigued by espionage and spies. I think he would put it somewhere that seemed like something a spy might do."

She continued to look around the room. She and Hawk checked a few places that seemed likely, but nothing. After about fifteen minutes, her eyes landed on an air vent at the top of the wall in a bedroom.

"Hawk, I think that's it."

Hawk looked at the air vent. She could be on to something. He pulled a chair over and climbed up so he could reach the vent. Carefully, he removed the cover and reached inside. He couldn't believe it when he pulled out a flash drive.

With quiet excitement, Cassie exclaimed, "You found it!"

Hawk smiled. "No, you found it. I just retrieved it."

Steven's voice came over the phone. "Guys, it doesn't really matter who found it. Now that you have it, get out of there."

"We're leaving now." He turned to Cassie as he stuck the drive in his pocket. "Let's get out of here."

"Gladly."

They quickly made their way down the hall and back down the three flights of stairs. Hawk wished the truck was closer to the back door, but he had parked it as close as he could. He opened the apartment building door and scanned the surrounding area. Reaching for Cassie's hand, they stepped outside. Almost instantly, a bullet whizzed past Cassie's head. Hawk pushed her to the ground and pulled her back inside the building.

Looking at Cassie, Hawk asked, "Are you all right?"

"I'm fine. Was someone shooting at us?"

"Yes." He spoke into his phone, "Steven, what's going on?"

"We have a shooter on the top of the adjacent building. We've got him covered. When I give you the go ahead, get her out of there. You two get in the truck and get out of here. We've got this covered."

Hawk looked at Cassie, and she nodded her understanding. She knew, when Steven gave the word, they would have to run, literally, for their lives.

In just a few seconds, Steven came back on. "We're ready. Stay low and get to the truck as fast as you can. Are you two ready?"

Hawk squeezed Cassie's hand. "We're ready."

Steven spoke to Cassie, "Cas, I love you, hon."

With tears in her eyes, Cassie replied, "I love you too, Steven."

Hawk eased the door open and looked back at Cassie, "Ready?"

She nodded her head. "Ready."

He pushed the door open, and they made a run for the truck. Gunfire erupted around them. Hawk jerked the truck door open and quickly jumped in behind Cassie. He turned the key and hit reverse. He rapidly backed out of the alley, jerked the truck into drive, and sped down the street, away from the gunfire.

After about ten minutes, he finally asked, "Are you okay?"

With obvious emotion in her voice, Cassie answered, "Yes. Are you?"

"Yes."

"When can we call Steven? I need to know he's okay."

Hawk knew it shouldn't matter, but he wondered what the relationship really was between Cassie and Steven. They both claimed they were just friends, but her concern seemed much deeper than mere friendship.

"He'll call us. Right now, we need to decide where we're going to go. We can't go back to my house. It may have been compromised."

Cassie instantly had a thought. "We could go to my parents' ranch. It's about twenty miles outside of town."

"That might work, but we can't risk putting your family in danger."

"They're not there. I would never suggest going there if they were. They are in Colorado and won't be back until the end of the month."

"Well, it could work. We need to let Steven know where we are, but I need to tell him without being specific, just in case our phones are being tracked."

"Just tell him Rocky Top. He'll understand."

Hawk nodded his head. Yes, he just felt there was something more than just friendship between Cassie and Steven. Cassie gave him directions to her parents, and he headed in that direction.

About ten minutes out, Cassie thought about Hank. "Hawk, I need to call Hank."

"Who's Hank?"

"He's my parents' neighbor. He's been taking care of the animals while they're away. He doesn't usually come up to the house, but if he sees lights on, he might come to check it out. I don't want him coming around the house…just in case."

Hawk didn't need her to explain her "just in case." He handed her his phone, and she punched in Hank's number.

"Hank, this is Cassie Marshall. I'm fine, thanks. Listen, I just wanted to let you know that I'm going to be staying at my parents' house for a few days, and I didn't want you to become concerned if you noticed lights on. No, everything is fine. I'm just working on a piece and need a quiet place to work for a few days. No, I have everything I need. But I know, if I need anything, I can give you a call. I will. Thanks, Hank." She punched the phone off and handed it back to Hawk.

"Everything okay with the neighbor?"

"Yes. Hank's a good man. He's always been great to take care of the animals when my parents are away."

They sat silently for several more minutes, but Hawk kept glancing at Cassie. She was being really strong, but he could tell she was still shaken from the shooting at the apartment building.

"Cassie, we can find another place to go if you don't want to risk staying at your parents' house."

"No, it will be fine. Hopefully, we'll be able to check out that drive and see what's on it."

Hawk just nodded his head in agreement but said nothing more. Ten minutes later, Cassie directed him to make a left turn at the next drive. He turned onto a long tree-lined, curved driveway leading up to a large ranch house. He looked out into the fields and saw cattle, sheep, and horses. There were also a couple of fields with crops, maybe beans and corn, but he couldn't really tell from this distance.

"This is a large ranch. Are there workers?"

"There are, but while my parents are away, they get a couple of weeks off. Hank and a couple of his workers will handle everything until my parents return at the end of the month."

Cassie understood his concern. Anyone on the ranch could be in danger. The fewer people that knew she was here, the better.

Hawk pulled up and stopped in front of the garage. As soon as he parked, his phone rang.

"Hawk, are you two okay?" Steven barely gave him time to answer before talking.

"Yes, we're fine. How about you and the rest of the officers?"

"Everybody's fine. We didn't catch the assailant, though. He somehow managed to escape."

"Not surprising. I'm sure he had his escape well planned out."

"I know, but it's still so frustrating. So where are you?"

"Cassie said to tell you we're at Rocky Top."

Steven knew instantly they were at the ranch. That was their childhood name for it. He also knew no one would be around right now since this was the month her parents and the ranch hands always went on vacation.

"Awesome. Just be careful. I'll be in touch soon."

"Okay. We will."

"So Steven and everybody is okay?"

"Yes, thank God everyone is okay."

He and Cassie got out and walked up to the front porch. Cassie reached under a flowerpot and retrieved a key which she used to unlock the door.

Once inside, Hawk told her he would open the garage door and pull the truck inside. "I'll be right back."

Cassie flipped on some lights and made her way to the back of the house. She walked over to the windows in the sunroom and looked out at the fields and pastures. Suddenly, the reality of the last few days hit her. As she stood there, she could no longer hold back the tears. That's where Hawk found her when he returned.

He stood for a minute as he watched her crying, and he could no longer hold himself back. He walked over to her and quietly said her name, "Cassie." He reached out and stroked her long auburn hair.

Cassie turned to face him, tears still rolling down her face. Hawk reached out and tenderly wiped the tears from her cheek. He cupped her face as he moved closer. Slowly, his lips met hers in a warm, tender kiss. Gradually, the kiss became more passionate as Cassie's arms went around Hawk's waist, holding him close. The desire and need that had been growing between them finally escaped in the power of that kiss.

When he eventually pulled away, Hawk continued to caress her face as he softly spoke, "It's going to be okay, Cassie. We're going to be okay." He tenderly kissed her again as he continued to caress her face. "I'm going to go check out the house. Will you be all right?"

Cassie nodded her head as she quietly answered, "I'll be fine."

Hawk turned and left the room. Cassie was in disbelief at what just happened. She knew her feelings for Hawk had been growing, but apparently, his had been growing too. She had been kissed many times, but never, never had she felt like that when a man had kissed her. Things just got a lot more complicated.

After checking out all the exits and potential safe spots in the house, Hawk returned to the kitchen to find Cassie making them something to eat.

"Everything look okay?"

"Yes. I mentally mapped us out a couple of escape plans…just in case. Can I help with anything?"

"There are some plates in the pie safe if you would like to get out a couple. I thought we could have some soup and grilled cheese. Does that sound okay?"

"Sounds wonderful." He got a couple of small plates and placed them on the kitchen island.

Cassie placed a bowl of soup beside each plate then put the sandwiches on the plates as they sat down to eat.

Hawk took a bite of his sandwich. "So is this where you grew up?"

"Most of my life, yes. We moved here when I was five. It was the week after Thanksgiving. I didn't want to leave Colorado and my grandparents and cousins, so going to a new school where I knew no one was extra difficult for me."

"Is that when you met Steven?"

A smile crossed Cassie's face. "Yes. I was hiding behind my parents, not wanting to go into the classroom. The teacher was doing her best to coax me in, but I wasn't having it. Then, this boy walked up and said, 'Hi, my name is Stevie. What's yours?' I just stood there. The teacher told him my name was Cassie. He said, 'Hi, Cassie. We're going to be friends. Come meet everybody.' He took my hand, and I never looked back. We've been friends ever since."

There was his opening. "So has there ever been anything romantic between the two of you?"

"No. He's always been like a brother to me." She laughed. "A very protective brother." She looked into Hawk's steel-blue eyes and held his gaze. "I love Steven…but as family. Nothing more. And he feels the same way about me."

Hawk placed his hand on top of Cassie's hand as he smiled. "That's good to know."

Once Cassie caught her breath, she asked him a question, "So why 'Hawk'? Surely that isn't a given name."

He laughed. "No, definitely not a given name. My parents named me Timothy Marcus, but I've been Hawk since I was eleven years old."

"Okay, now I have to know the story."

He smiled. "It's actually a pretty good story. When I was eleven, my brother and I were playing in our backyard when our dog suddenly took off into the woods. We lived in an area much like this. It was a rural area, surrounded by woods. My brother was seven at the time, and that dog was his best friend. He was afraid something would happen to him in the woods, so he took off after him. Of course, I was afraid something would happen to my brother, so I took off after him. I'm not sure how long we ran, but there was no sign of our dog anywhere. It started getting dark, and I realized we were lost. I had no idea how to get back home. There was a cave close by, so we crawled inside for the night."

Hawk took a deep breath as though the next part of his story was going to take a little extra. "As soon as the sun started coming up, I looked out and prayed that God would show us how to get home. I heard a bird and looked up to see a red-tailed hawk perched in a tree beside the cave. He was looking straight at me. In that instant, it was like God told me, 'Follow the hawk.' The hawk took off flying, and I grabbed my brother's hand, and we followed the hawk. When it lighted in a tree, I was like 'Now what?' As if in response, I heard another hawk. I looked to my right, and there was another red-tailed hawk. When it took flight, so did we. That happened four more times. The last hawk landed in a tree in our backyard."

"Wow. I have goose bumps."

"Yeah, it's a pretty cool story. My dad asked us how we managed to find our way home, and my brother told him I followed the hawks. Ever since that day, I have been called Hawk."

"That's so cool."

"Yes, it is."

"So did you find your dog?"

Hawk laughed at her question. "He was waiting for us in the backyard. Our family and neighbors had gathered and were forming search parties, and there was Rex right in the middle of it all." He knew it was time to get down to business even though he would rather continue to escape from their current reality. "Well, how about we clean up this mess and go see if we can run this flash drive on your father's laptop."

Ten minutes later, they were in her father's office, flash drive inserted into the laptop.

Chapter 8

Cassie typed in her father's password, and Hawk sat down at the desk in front of the laptop. At first, it looked as though there was nothing on the drive. Then, there it was.

With a gasp, Cassie looked at the information that was coming up on the screen. "Is that what I think it is?"

Hawk couldn't believe his eyes—or their luck. "If you think it is the nail in Espinoza's coffin, then, yes, it's exactly what you think it is."

He scrolled through the information, and he knew they had him. There were phony ledgers, records of drug deals, numerous bank accounts in various countries, and even payoffs for murders for hire.

Cassie was in disbelief. "How did Carson possibly get this?"

Hawk shook his head. "I don't know, but this is not a copy. It's the original flash drive. This has to be what Espinoza is after."

"But I didn't have it. Why is he after me?"

"My guess would be that's why Carson deceived you at the warehouse. He was apparently working with Espinoza and, somehow, got his hands on the flash drive. When Espinoza discovered the drive was missing, Carson knew he had to do something. He probably planned to frame you to get the suspicion off himself." He saw the tears welling in Cassie's eyes.

"I just can't believe he would do that to me. We weren't really close, but we were friends. He had to know that Espinoza would kill me."

Hawk gently touched her face. "I don't think he intended for it to get that far. He did try to stop Espinoza's man from killing you and possibly saved your life by shielding you and slowing the bullet

41

with his own body. He obviously underestimated the man he was up against. Or overestimated his own abilities. Either way, it cost him his life." He tenderly kissed Cassie and then looked into her moist eyes. "I'm not going to let him get to you, Cassie. I promise."

Cassie placed her hand gently on his face. "But what if protecting me costs you your life? I don't think I could bear anything happening to you."

Hawk knew, at that moment, without a doubt, he was falling in love with Cassandra Marshall. He met her lips with his and took her in a deep, passionate kiss that left them both weak and breathless.

Finally, he softly spoke, "Nothing's going to happen to either of us. God has brought us together, and He's going to get us safely out of this. We're going to make it, Cassie." He held up the flash drive. "We have what we need to get out of this. So I say we put an end to this once and for all."

Cassie took a deep breath as she looked into his warm steel-blue eyes and knew, undoubtedly, that she could trust this man with her life. "Okay, what do we do next?"

"I get this drive to Steven so he can get it to my team and Espinoza can finally be arrested. Did I see a gun safe in the garage?" He thought he saw Cassie tense but assumed it was because of the implications presented by this flash drive.

With obvious hesitation in her voice, Cassie answered, "Yes, that's my father's gun safe."

"Do you have a key to it?"

"I know where it is. Why?"

"We need to be sure we have ourselves well armed. I want us to be prepared for anything."

"You want me to have a gun?"

No, there was no doubt. Cassie had a look of fear at the mention of the guns. Something was going on.

"Cassie, I need to know you are able to defend yourself while I'm gone."

Panic lit Cassie's face. "Gone! What do you mean?"

Hawk tried to calmly relate the details and relieve her sudden panic. "I told you. I need to get this drive to Steven, ASAP."

"Well, I can just go with you."

Hawk heard the fear in her voice, and he hated what she was going through right now.

"The last time you came with me, you almost got killed. It's not safe for you to go with me. You'll be safer here. I'll only be gone for an hour or less. As far as we know, Espinoza doesn't have this place on his radar yet, so you should be safe here. But just in case, I want you to have a gun to defend yourself, if necessary. Can you shoot a gun?"

With an obvious tremble in her voice, Cassie softly answered, "Yes. I guess I still can. It's been a while."

She was still struggling. Hawk needed to know why.

"Cassie, what's going on? Why is this an issue? Tell me what's bothering you."

Cassie was breathing hard, and he could see the pain in her eyes.

She stood silently for several minutes and then quietly responded, "I haven't touched a gun in ten years."

He gently caressed her arm as he softly asked, "Why, Cassie? What happened ten years ago?"

Tears floated in her eyes as her thoughts went back to ten years earlier.

"My father had taken my three brothers, my sister, and me hunting. We had gone on hunting trips for years, so we were all used to guns and knew how to use them safely. We had three deer stands. My father and oldest brother were in one deer stand. My sister and middle brother were in a deer stand. And my youngest brother, Tad, and I were in a deer stand. We had been in the field for a couple of hours. I don't really remember exactly what happened next. Tad was helping me with something…and his gun fell out of the deer stand." Cassie closed her eyes as the tears rolled down her face.

Hawk pulled her close and held her in his arms as he kissed the side of her head. He wiped the tears from her face as she continued.

"When the gun hit the ground, it went off. The bullet came up into our deer stand and hit Tad in the chest. They said he died instantly."

Hawk closed his eyes as he suddenly realized her pain and held her tighter. "Honey, I'm so sorry. I can't imagine how very difficult that was for you."

"I haven't been able to touch a gun since that day. If he hadn't been helping me…"

Hawk gently touched her face as he looked into her moist brown eyes. "Cassie, you have to know it wasn't your fault. It was just a terrible, terrible accident. I didn't know your brother, but if he was anything like you, I know he wouldn't want you carrying this burden around with you."

"I know. My family has said the same to me. And I don't blame myself. But I still have an unshakable fear of holding a gun."

"Cassie, honey, I totally get that. But it's not safe for you to go with me, and I can't leave you here defenseless. I need you to try to overcome this fear. Do you think you can try?"

Cassie knew he was right. She also knew it was time to get her life back. She nodded her head. Quietly, she stood and went to her parents' room and got the key to the gun safe. She came back and handed the key to Hawk. Without speaking, he gently took her hand in his, and they walked to the garage.

Hawk unlocked the gun safe and pulled out a couple of rifles, two handguns, and some ammunition.

He loaded all the guns then looked at Cassie. "Are you going to be okay with this?"

"I'll be fine." She reached for one of the handguns. "It's time to reclaim my life."

Hawk smiled as he tenderly touched her face. "You are an amazing woman, Cassie Marshall. I'll call Steven and make arrangements to get the drive to him."

"I think I'll go wait for you in the sunroom."

After she was gone, Hawk called Steven. "Hey, man. We hit the motherload."

"Are you serious? The flash drive?"

"It has everything on it. Espinoza won't walk away from this. I need to get the drive to you so you can deliver it to DEA headquarters. I can't leave Cassie unprotected until Espinoza is in custody, so I can't risk being gone very long. Where can we meet?"

"There's a park about five miles from the ranch."

"McKinnly. Yeah, I know it."

"I can be there in about thirty minutes."

"Call me when you're about five minutes out, and I'll meet you there."

Steven suddenly realized Hawk wasn't saying "we." "Wait, are you planning on leaving Cassie alone?"

"I'll only be gone for twenty to thirty minutes. And she'll be armed so she can defend herself should it be necessary. But it won't be necessary. She'll be safer staying than coming with me. At least if something happens to me, she'll still stand a chance."

"Well, that's a cheery thought. Did you say she will be armed? Armed with what?"

"With one of her father's handguns and a rifle."

"You can't be serious? Have you talked to her? Does she know what you are planning to do?"

"Yes, I have, and yes, she does. Steven, she told me about her brother."

"She...what? She never talks about Tad. It's too painful for her. And she hasn't touched a gun since the accident."

"I know. But she said it was time to get her life back. She's fine, Steven. I know I don't have to tell you what a strong woman she is."

"No, you don't have to tell me. If she's finally opening up and overcoming the weight she's been bearing for the last ten years, that's all that matters. Apparently, you've been able to do what her family and I have been trying unsuccessfully to do for a decade. You must be doing something right. I'll meet you at the park in about a half hour."

"I'll see you there. And, Steven...watch your back."

"You do the same."

Hawk joined Cassie in the sunroom.

"I poured you a cup of coffee."

He picked up the cup as he sat down on the couch beside Cassie. "Thanks. I'm meeting Steven in about thirty minutes at the park to give him the drive."

Cassie sat very still, not responding to anything Hawk was saying. She didn't really know what to say.

He sat down his coffee cup and turned to face her, placing his hand gently on her face. As she looked up into his steel-blue eyes, he saw the tears pooling in her eyes.

He spoke to her softly, "Cassie, I'll only be gone for twenty minutes, thirty at the most. I'll be back before you even know I'm gone."

She locked her soft brown eyes on his. "I'm not worried about me. I'm worried about you. What if something happens to you? I just don't know if I…" Cassie let the sentence die.

"Nothing is going to happen to me, Cassie. I'll be back here safe and sound in a half hour."

His phone rang, and he saw that it was Steven.

"It's Steven." He answered, "Okay, I'm on my way." He put the phone in his pocket as he stood and pulled Cassie to her feet. He pulled her close and wrapped his arms protectively around her. "I have to go. I'll be back before you know it. Keep the doors locked and the blinds and curtains pulled. And don't go anywhere without that gun. We're going to be fine."

He wiped the tears from her face and kissed her long and tenderly. With one last look and a final glance into those warm brown eyes, he turned and left to meet with Steven.

Chapter 9

Hawk had only been gone for a few minutes, but to Cassie, it felt like hours. This was her childhood home. She knew every nook and cranny of this house. But right now, she jumped at every creak and groan. She walked through the house, checking all the windows and doors, even though she knew Hawk had checked everything twice before he left. She finally walked into the dining room. There was one large window at the front of the room. But the blinds were closed, so no one could see inside. Walking over to the table, she sat on the chair at the end of the table. It was against the back wall, so there were no doors or windows behind her. No one could come up behind her.

Walking through the house had wreaked havoc on her nerves. She sat at the table with the gun sitting in front of her and began to think of Bible verses.

I will not fear tho tens of thousands assail me. The Lord is my light and salvation, whom shall I fear? The Lord is the stronghold of my life, of whom shall I be afraid? But I will rescue you on that day, declares the Lord. You will not be given into the hands of those you fear. What time I am afraid, I will trust in You.

Cassie realized she must be more afraid than she thought. All the verses that came to mind had to do with fear.

"Lord, what have I gotten myself into? Please protect Hawk, Steven, me, everyone who is trying to stop Enrique Espinoza. He's an evil man, Lord. But I know You have overcome evil. Don't let him win."

The sound of footsteps in the hall brought Cassie's thoughts to a sudden stop. She started to call out Hawk's name but realized, if it was Hawk, the footsteps wouldn't be so slow and he would have identified himself. Cassie was instantly alert as she picked up the handgun on the table and aimed it at the doorway.

Hawk pulled into the park where he found Steven waiting for him. He got out of the car and walked toward Steven. Pulling out the flash drive, he handed it to Steven.

"This is the nail. We weren't able to read everything because some of it is encrypted. But the tech people should be able to decode it. Even without it, though, there's enough on there to put Espinoza away for good."

"I'll get it to DEA headquarters now. But we may have a problem."

"What kind of problem?"

"One of our clerks was found dead, murdered, yesterday. We think it was probably Espinoza."

"Why do you say that?"

"We started digging and found there had been four $20,000 deposits into her savings account over the last month. She works for the SMPD. We don't make that kind of money."

"So Espinoza was paying her. For what? Information?"

"That's our guess. I know you and I are the only ones who know where you and Cassie are right now. But it's always possible she could have found out. We're still digging, but in the meantime, your location may have been compromised."

"You mean Espinoza might know where Cassie is?"

"Not likely, but possible."

"I've got to get back." As he hurried back to his truck, he relayed the contact information to Steven. "Get that drive to Reed Duncan at DEA. Call him on the way and let him know you're coming." As he jumped into his truck, he yelled, "And have him send a team to the ranch. Fast."

"Call me when you get back!"

Hawk waved his hand out the window in response and then sped down the road at full speed.

Cassie listened as the footsteps came closer. Slowly, she stood with her back against the wall and aimed the gun at the doorway. With the sound of each step, her heart pounded a little harder. She was amazed that her hand was steady. Her eyes were glued to the dining room entryway as one of Espinoza's men stepped around and aimed his gun directly at her.

The man smiled coldly as he looked at her. "Well, that didn't take long. Now, just put that gun down and come with me."

With a steady voice, her eyes never wavering, she replied, "That's not going to happen."

"Oh, it's going to happen, or I'll drop you where you stand." He slowly continued to move toward Cassie.

"If you take another step, I'll shoot."

"I don't think so." He kept coming toward her.

Cassie yelled, "I said stop!"

He laughed and took another step. Cassie pulled the trigger.

Hawk couldn't explain the feeling he had, but something didn't feel right. As he neared the drive to the ranch, he pulled his truck over and parked on the side of the road. He got out of the truck, grabbed his guns and night goggles, and then hurried to the woods that ran adjacent to the Marshall ranch.

About twenty yards into the woods, he heard footsteps to his left. Quickly, he ducked into some underbrush and watched as two men came closer. Both men were carrying AK-47s. And they were headed toward the house. Hawk knew he could take them both out without any problem. But he didn't know how many more there might be, and he didn't want to alert them to his presence. He knew he needed to get to the house before they did. As soon as they were clear of his location, he took off to the right to circle around behind the house.

There was another man standing at the back door to the house, so he couldn't get in that way. He hadn't seen anyone else, so he was hoping and praying that these three men were all Espinoza had sent. Carefully, he made his way to the side door of the garage and quietly opened it as he made his way inside. He had just closed the door when he heard a gunshot from inside the house.

Cassie!

He knew the man standing guard at the back door would probably rush in at the sound of a gunshot. So he quickly pushed the kitchen door open and immediately aimed his gun on the back door.

As expected, the guard rushed inside. Hawk shot him before he had time to fully get into the house. Then he turned to go and find Cassie.

Cassie slowly lowered the gun as she looked at the dead body lying on her parents' dining room floor. She was amazed that she wasn't scared, but she shouldn't have been. After all, she had been reciting scripture and praying for the last half hour. She knew the man had to be with Espinoza. What she didn't know was how he possibly found them. And she realized he probably wasn't alone. She was about to leave the dining room and go to the hidden closet when she heard a gunshot come from the direction of the kitchen.

Who could possibly be shooting? They wouldn't be shooting at each other.

Hawk... He had to be back.

She moved slowly to the front of the dining room in hopes of seeing Hawk coming from the kitchen.

Hawk made his way down the hall to the main dining room. He knew that would be the safest room in which to wait and that was probably where Cassie had gone. As he neared the room, he saw the body of a man lying in the doorway. He slowed down and, with gun drawn, quietly made his way toward the dining room. He was almost to the doorway when he caught sight of someone moving. He aimed his gun and carefully proceeded the remaining few feet. Just as he reached the doorway, he caught Cassie's reflection in the glass in the hall clock.

"Cassie, it's Hawk. Are you okay?"

"I'm fine. I'm coming out." She quickly stepped from the room and was pulled into a quick embrace from Hawk.

He stepped back and took her by the arm and headed back down the hall toward the kitchen. "We don't have much time. There were at least two more men outside. They had to have heard the gunshots and will be here any second. Let's see if we can get back to the garage. If they are the only other men here, we might be able to escape through the side door of the garage."

Cassie saw the other dead body in the kitchen as they hurried to the garage. She knew she was definitely in way over her head. They made it to the garage just as the other two men rushed in the back door. There were some boxes and a large tool box against the side wall which Hawk had arranged before going to meet Steven. He had pulled them out just enough for him and Cassie to squeeze behind them, yet from the door, they appeared to be against the wall. He pulled Cassie down with him now and prayed Espinoza's men wouldn't come looking or, even worse, that they wouldn't just aim their assault rifles and just start shooting up everything.

Within minutes, they heard the kitchen door open to the garage. Cassie remained silently huddled behind Hawk, praying non-stop. They could hear at least one of the men coming down the steps into the garage. Hawk knelt with his gun ready, hoping they would not find their hiding place. They could hear the footsteps walking quickly around the garage, and then they hurried back up the steps and into the house.

Hawk and Cassie remained silent and still for several more minutes. Finally, Hawk motioned for Cassie to stay hidden and he was going to see if the coast was clear. Cautiously, he stepped from their hiding place and carefully surveyed the garage. No one was there. He made his way over to the front window and glanced outside. There was no sign of anyone. He went to the side door and very slowly cracked it open. He, again, saw no one. He stood and listened for a few minutes but heard no one either. Slowly he opened the door enough to look around it, but the men appeared to be gone, and there was no one else there. He looked toward their hiding place and motioned for Cassie to join him.

Cassie quickly made her way to Hawk's side. Part of him wanted to stay where they were, but he knew they had been compromised and it was quite possible more men could be on their way. They had to leave.

"We're going to make a run for the woods at the back of the house. Are you okay to do that?"

"I'm fine. Are all the men gone?"

"It appears so. At least, for now. I want you to run in front of me. I'll be right on your back. Are you ready?"

Cassie nodded her head.

Hawk pulled her in front of him and, in a loud whisper, said, "Go!"

Chapter 10

Cassie and Hawk ran into the woods and kept running for what seemed like hours. When they reached the creek, they sat down on a fallen tree trunk to rest and regroup.

Hawk reached down and took Cassie's hand in his. "I think we're safe for now, but we're going to need to find somewhere to hide." He reached up and tenderly stroked her face. "Are you doing okay?"

"As okay as I can be. I'm just glad you're okay. I was so scared when I heard that gunshot. I was afraid you had been shot."

He continued to stroke her cheek. "I thought the same thing about you." He smiled slightly at her. "You were amazing back there. I think I'm pretty glad I have you on my side."

"Let's hope that doesn't change. You said we needed somewhere to hide. I think I may know a place."

"Okay. Is it far?"

"Not too far. If we follow the creek and go up the mountain a little piece, we will find a cave. My brothers and sister and I used to play in it when we were younger. Steven and his brothers did too. We could hide there for a while, at least until we decide what to do next."

"That's a good idea. Is it a confined cave, or does it have an exit?"

"There's another opening all the way through the cave. You have to climb up a little to reach it, but it opens up into the field at the back of the neighbor's ranch."

"Sounds like it might just work. I'll let you lead the way since you know how to get there. Are you ready to head up the mountain?"

"I'm ready."

Hawk stood and pulled Cassie to her feet. Hand in hand, they started the hike up the mountain. After about thirty minutes, they reached the cave.

"Well, here it is."

Hawk suddenly had a thought that should have occurred to him when Cassie mentioned the cave. Obviously, he wasn't thinking as clearly as he should be. "We have one problem. How are we going to see once we get in the cave? We don't have any kind of light with us."

"Well, maybe we do." Cassie walked over to the cave opening and reached inside. She stepped back out holding a lantern and a tin can. "It's been a long time, but maybe these will still work."

Hawk smiled. "I take it you must have come here often."

Cassie laughed. "We were a pretty adventurous group of kids. Plus it was a good make-out spot when we were teenagers."

With a twinkle in his eye, Hawk replied, "I'll have to keep that in mind."

He took the lantern, which amazingly still had oil in it, and rolled up the wick. Cassie handed him a match from the tin can, and he struck it against a rock and then lit the wick.

"Looks like we have light. Let's get inside and see if we can make our way to the other end."

Reed Duncan and his team converged on the Marshall ranch to an eerily quiet scene. They had spotted Hawk's truck parked at the edge of the road. Parking their vehicles in the same area, they quickly exited them, and Duncan rushed into action. He dispersed his four agents, and they cautiously moved toward the house. Eventually, they made their way inside the house where they discovered two dead cartel members and no sign of Hawk Logan or Cassandra Marshall.

Reed called his captain to fill him in on the situation. "Yes, sir, that's right. No, there is no sign of Logan or Ms. Marshall. I don't know where they went, but we'll figure it out."

"I might be able to help with that."

Reed turned to see Steven Hollister standing in the doorway. "I'll get back to you, Captain. I think we may have just gotten our first lead." He hung up his phone. "Hollister. What are you doing here?"

"I just had a bad feeling and decided to check it out. Guess it's a good thing I did."

Reed could certainly use some help right now, but he wasn't sure this was where he wanted it to come from. He wasn't fond of working with local law enforcement. But right now, he appeared to have no other choice.

"Okay. So how do you think you can help find Hawk and the girl?"

Steven didn't like Duncan's attitude toward Cassie. "That 'girl' happens to be a very good friend of mine, not just a pawn in some game you're playing."

"Look, I'm sorry. I didn't mean any disrespect. Hawk happens to be a good friend of mine too. Right now, I just want to find the two of them before Espinoza's men do. What do you have?"

"There's a cave up the mountain. It has an exit that comes out in an adjacent field. I think that's where they may have gone. We can circle around to the backfield and come up at the exit. If they're in that cave, they will come out that exit."

"Okay, it's the best we have for now. Let's head up and hope we're not too late."

Cassie knew they should be getting close to the exit. "It should be right around the next corner. But we should be seeing some light and feeling some air. Neither of those are happening."

Hawk could sense the panic building in Cassie's voice. "It could be anything. Let's just keep going. You said we're almost there."

They came around the curve in the cave and discovered why there was no air blowing and no light.

"Oh, no. Now what?"

Duncan and his agents followed Steven up the mountain road for about a mile. He came to a stop at the edge of an opening in the woods and exited his truck.

Duncan and the agents pulled over behind him. "Why are we stopping? I don't see any cave here."

Steven pointed up the path at the edge of the opening. "It's a few feet up this trail. We can't drive. We have to walk."

Duncan glanced up at the steep path. "All right. Let's go."

Ten minutes later, they reached the cave opening. But the sight that met them was not what they wanted to see.

"Hawk, what are we going to do?"

The opening to the outside was blocked by rocks. Apparently, there had been a rockslide at some point over the past few years, and the rocks had lodged into the opening and blocked the exit.

Hawk took a deep breath and tried to think. "Let's not panic just yet. Let me see if I can get any of the rocks to move."

Cassie put her hand on his arm. "Wait! What if they fall through the opening? They could fall on you. You could be hurt. I'm not sure this is a good idea."

Hawk placed his hand on top of Cassie's. "I'll be careful, but we have to try. Just stand back some while I try."

Reluctantly, Cassie stepped back out of the way—and prayed.

Hawk climbed up and pushed on the rocks, but they didn't budge. He knew it was a long shot, but he had to try. The rocks would have to be moved from the outside.

Steven rushed to the opening that was now covered with rocks. There had been some extremely heavy rains in the mountains a few years earlier that had caused flooding and landslides. The rocks now covering the opening must be a result of those rains.

"Come on! Help me move these rocks!" He began taking rocks off the pile and tossing them aside.

Duncan wasn't so sure this was necessary. "Wait, we don't even know they're in the cave. This could be a total waste of time."

"They're in there. I know it." He continued to dig. "Come on, Duncan. Give me a hand. They can't risk going back out the other end. If Espinoza's men followed them, they'll be waiting for them."

"Okay, we'll help. But I still think this could all be a total waste of time." He nodded to his team, and they all pitched in to remove the stones.

Hawk and Cassie sat down on a rock as he pulled her into his arms and kissed the top of her head.

"We'll get out, Cassie, even if we have to go back to the other end."

Cassie laid her head on his shoulder. "But we can't do that, can we? If we go back that way, Espinoza's men could be waiting for us."

Hawk knew she was right. They had no other option. They were going to somehow have to move those rocks—and soon. If Espinoza's men found the cave, they weren't likely to wait outside long for them to come out. They would eventually come in after them.

"I'll try the rocks again. If I could find one that is loose, maybe it will dislodge the others."

Cassie placed her hand softly on his face. "So they could fall on you? Hawk, I don't want anything to happen to you."

"I have to try, honey. I have to get you out of here and somewhere safe."

She sat up. "Okay, but I'm going to help."

"Cassie, your arm is still healing. You don't need to be moving these rocks with you arm."

"I'll just use my other arm, promise."

She smiled that gorgeous smile, and he couldn't refuse.

"Okay, but just your good arm."

They once again began to push and pull on the rocks. But this time, they heard someone on the other side. Problem was, Who was it?

"Stop! Wait, wait!"

"What's up, Hollister?"

"There's someone on the other side. I can hear movement." He bent close to the rocks where they had moved some away and yelled, "Hawk? Cassie? Can you hear me? Hawk!"

Hawk stopped pushing the rocks and put his hand on Cassie's arm. "Did you hear that?"

Cassie nodded her head. "Was that Steven?"

Hawk yelled up through the rocks, "Steven! Steven, it's Hawk. Can you hear me?"

"I hear you! Listen, move away from the opening. Duncan and his team are here helping. We'll get the rocks moved, but they might fall in as we move them. Is Cassie all right?"

Cassie answered, "I'm fine, Steven. Just get us out."

"We will."

Hawk and Cassie moved away from the opening; and Steven, Duncan, and the other men quickly got back to work, moving the rocks away from the opening.

After several minutes, light started seeping through the small opening they had made, and fresh air began to fill the cave. Hawk noticed excessive dust falling from the rocks and somehow knew they were about to fall. He grabbed Cassie's hand and pulled her with him around the corner just as a huge pile of large rocks plummeted to the cave floor.

Before the dust even cleared, Steven was yelling into the opening, "Hawk! Cassie!"

Coughing, Hawk replied, "We're okay. Now, let's get out of here."

Steven and Reed both breathed a sigh of relief and lifted a quick prayer of gratitude.

Steven looked at the hole that had been opened. "The hole is as large as we're going to be able to get it without equipment. The rest of the rocks are packed in tight."

Hawk inspected the opening. "We can make it. I'll lift Cassie out then climb up. I can probably only make it halfway. Someone will have to reach down and help pull me the rest of the way out."

"Let's do it. Go ahead and send Cassie out."

Hawk gently touched Cassie's face and then met her lips with a deep, heart-stopping kiss. "Are you ready?"

She smiled into those strong steel-blue eyes. "After that kiss, I think I could conquer the world."

He gave a little laugh. "Let's get you out of here first. Then we'll worry about conquering the world. You were a cheerleader in high school, weren't you?"

"Yes, but how…"

With a smile, he answered, "Lucky guess. I'm going to bend down, and I need you to stand on my shoulders. Steven will be able to reach in and lift you out."

"But how are you going to get out?"

"By the grace of God. Now, climb up." He bent down, and Cassie easily climbed onto his strong shoulders. Hawk held tightly to her legs. "Okay, Steven! Pull her out!"

Cassie reached toward the opening, and Steven reached down and found her hands. She tightened her grip around his wrists, and he carefully pulled her out of the cave. The instant she was out, Steven stepped aside and pulled her into his arms.

"I was so worried. Are you all right? You're not hurt, are you?"

"No, I'm fine. We need to get Hawk out, though."

Steven nodded toward the opening. "They're already on it."

Reed was halfway down into the hole while two of the other agents held his feet to keep him from falling in. It was going to take all of them to lift Hawk out. He was well over six feet tall and quite muscular. He wouldn't be an easy haul.

Hawk stood on the large boulder that was directly under the opening and reached up as high as he could. He was barely able to reach Reed's hands. It was a good thing both men were so tall, or this might not have worked. Reed grabbed Hawk's wrists, and Hawk did the same to Reed.

Reed yelled back to his men, "I've got him. Pull us out!"

Carefully and quickly, the two agents began to pull Reed back out of the opening. As soon as Reed was out and Hawk's hands were visible, the other two agents rushed to grab his hands and help get him out of the cave.

Steadying himself, Hawk looked at his friend and pulled him into a hug. "I owe you, man. Thanks."

Reed slapped Hawk's shoulder. "Glad we made it in time."

Cassie left the safety of Steven's embrace and ran to Hawk, throwing her arms around his neck. Hawk pulled her into a tight embrace and held on like he might never let go. Steven watched the exchange between his two friends and noticed that this wasn't just a friendly so-glad-you're-safe kind of hug. There was much more to that hug than just friendship.

Reed broke the moment by reminding them of the situation at hand. "Okay, we need to get on the road and get you two somewhere safe. We don't have any idea what Espinoza is up to or where his men are. But being out here in the open is definitely not a good idea."

Everyone agreed, and they quickly descended from the mountain back to their vehicles. The fact that Hawk held Cassie's hand all the way back to the cars did not go unnoticed by Steven.

They had three vehicles, so two agents took the lead car. The other two agents took the rear car; and Reed rode in the truck with Steven, Cassie, and Hawk. Reed got in on the passenger side beside Steven while Cassie and Hawk sat in the back. As they drove down the road, Steven glanced back several times and noticed that Cassie's fingers were tightly laced with Hawk's. Definitely more than just friendship.

About ten miles into the trip, they noticed a traffic jam on the highway ahead of them.

Hawk was on instant alert. "Stop the vehicles!"

The three vehicles were all in communication with each other, so at Hawk's response, they all began to slow down and pull to the side of the road.

Reed turned to face Hawk. "What's wrong? It's probably just a wreck or, possibly, construction."

Possibly, but Hawk's senses were on high alert after the last few days. And something about this just didn't feel right.

"Maybe, but I don't think so. We need to turn around and go the other way. I think it could be a trap."

Reed had worked with Hawk for five years, and one thing he had learned was that Hawk had amazingly keen instincts. If he said it didn't feel right, then something wasn't right.

"Okay, men, you heard him. Let's turn this convoy around and head the other direction."

But they never had a chance to even get the vehicles back on the road. There was a loud explosion, and the lead vehicle burst into flames. Steven's truck and the rear car both went airborne. Hawk's instincts had been right, but unfortunately, they weren't able to act fast enough.

Chapter 11

The sound of sirens and voices yelling orders rang in Hawk's ears. His head was pounding, and he fought to open his eyes. As he managed to force his eyes open, he looked around and tried to orient himself. How long had he been out? What happened? There was an explosion. The truck flew into the air. He looked at his hand. He had been holding Cassie's hand. It wasn't there.

With great effort, he managed to look around the truck. They were upside down. But the truck appeared to be intact, and the roof wasn't smashed in significantly. He looked toward the front seat. Steven and Reed were both unconscious and not moving.

Please, Lord, let them be alive.

Then fighting through the pain, he turned to his right to see if Cassie was all right. But when he looked in that direction, the door was standing open, and there was no sign of Cassie.

Weakly, he called her name, "Cassie. Cassie!"

He heard a voice call his name as a hand reached in and touched his shoulder. "Hawk. Hawk, can you hear me?"

Hawk managed to turn his head back toward the window. "Tanner? Tanner, are you okay?"

David Tanner was the agent who had been riding on the passenger side of the rear vehicle. "I have a broken arm, but I'm fine. Help is here, and we're going to get all of you out."

"Tanner, Cassie's gone. Did she fall out of the truck? Is she all right?"

"First responders are on scene, and everything is being handled. I'm going to get out of the way so they can work."

Hawk felt the blood streaming down his face, and his head was pounding with pain. But he wasn't so out of it that he didn't notice that Tanner didn't actually answer his question. Where was Cassie? Was she all right? She couldn't be dead.

No, please, God, don't let her be dead. I just found her. I can't lose her.

A firefighter came over to the vehicle to talk to Hawk. "Hawk, I'm Craig. We're going to get your friends in front out first then get you. So just hang tight. We're going to get you out as quickly as we can. Are you doing okay?"

"I'm fine. Where's Cassie? Have you found her? She was in the seat with me when we flipped, but she's not here now."

"We're taking care of everyone. We'll have you out in a few minutes."

Again, he didn't answer his question.

Lord, where's Cassie? Please, please, Lord, hold her close and keep her safe.

Hawk watched as they pulled Steven and Reed from the front of the truck. Reed had regained consciousness right before they pulled him out, but Steven appeared to still be unconscious. Once they were out, the firefighters came to the back to get him out. His door was jammed, so they had to use the Jaws of Life to rip it open. Hawk, however, wondered why that was necessary. The other door was standing wide open, and there was nothing blocking the path from his seat to the door. Couldn't they have just pulled him through the other door? His senses were on high alert again. Something, other than the obvious, was terribly wrong.

The paramedics were working on Steven and Reed and now began working on Hawk.

Tanner came over to check on him while the paramedic worked. "Hey, man. Are you okay?"

"I'm good. How are Reed and Steven?"

"From what I can gather, they will both be all right. Reed is pretty much like you. Gashed head and cuts and scrapes. Hollister seems a little worse, but he is conscious and talking. May have some internal injuries. Chopper is waiting to fly him out."

"And the others?"

Tanner took a deep breath. "McCray and Douglas were killed instantly when their car exploded. Winston is about like Hollister. He's being Life Flighted out now."

Hawk closed his eyes. *Two DEA agents dead and another apparently critical. And Steven. Lord, lay Your healing hands on my friend. Give him strength to endure and heal. Now, the main question, one more time.*

"Where's Cassie, Tanner? No one will tell me where she is."

Hawk didn't like the look on Tanner's face. "She's not here, Hawk."

"What do you mean she's not here? She has to be here."

"I'm sorry, Hawk, but she's not here."

Hawk started to get up, but the paramedic made him stay put. He looked up and saw Reed slowly making his way toward him. He sat down on the back of the truck beside Hawk.

"Reed, what's going on? Tanner says Cassie's not here. How can she be missing? She wouldn't just walk away."

"I've been talking to one of the troopers who was first on the scene. He said some of the people who were stopped in the traffic jam saw some men take someone out of the truck and carry them to a chopper that was waiting in the field."

Hawk couldn't believe what he was hearing. "Someone took Cassie? But why? That doesn't make sense. And it doesn't fit Espinoza's MO. What's going on here, Reed?"

Reed Duncan shook his head slowly. "I don't know, but we're going to figure this out."

Hawk was fuming. Despite his pain, he stood up and headed toward Steven who was being prepared to put on the medevac. He would find Cassie, but he had to know Steven was going to be all right. He stood by Steven and put his hand on his shoulder.

He looked like crap.

"Hey, man. You're going to be okay. Just be tough."

Steven looked at his friend and could see the pain in his eyes. It was a mixture of physical and emotional pain. "I'm going to be fine, but I'm out of commission for a while. I heard the troopers talking about Cassie. Someone took her out of the truck?"

"I'm going to find her. I'll bring her home, Steven. We're not going to lose her."

"I believe you will. Just be careful. I don't think we're dealing with just Espinoza."

"No, neither do I. I'll be careful. You just take care of yourself. I'm not bringing her home to find her best friend dead."

"I will." The paramedics were ready to load Steven on the chopper. "Hawk."

"Yeah."

"I'm good with you and Cassie. I can't think of anyone I would rather see her with."

"Thanks, man. That means a lot. Now, go get yourself patched up."

They loaded him on the medevac and took off.

Reed walked over and stood beside Hawk. "We'll find her, Hawk."

Hawk just watched as the chopper took flight, never looking at Reed. "That's why they cut me out instead of pulling me through the other side. They didn't want to risk damaging evidence. They're not going to find anything. We both know that."

"Probably not. But we still have lots of leads."

"Right now she's probably halfway to Mexico. With every minute we wait, her trail is getting colder."

"Hawk…"

"I'm going after her."

"To Mexico? Hawk, you know you don't have jurisdiction in Mexico. You would have to get authorization. There are agents in place who can follow the trail."

"They don't know what we know. They would have to catch up, and that is more precious time. I'm going."

"The captain will have your badge if you go off without proper authorization."

Hawk looked at his friend with no expression on his face to reveal his thoughts. He reached into his pocket and pulled out his ID badge and handed it to Reed. "He can have it. I don't need a badge to find her. I'm going back to the ranch to get her father's truck and heading to the airport."

"Hawk, don't go off half-cocked. Think this through. You won't even have a gun."

"There's nothing to think about. And I can get a gun after I get to Mexico. We both know how easy that is to do."

He walked over to one of the troopers, and Reed watched as he got in the car with the trooper and they headed back down the road toward the Marshall ranch.

Chapter 12

Hawk sat impatiently in the terminal, waiting for his flight to Mexico City, Mexico, to load. His thoughts were spinning so fast he couldn't even keep up with them. Why would Espinoza take Cassie? He had to know she didn't have the flash drive anymore. What could he possibly want? And who else was involved in all this? How deep did this all go? His thoughts were suddenly interrupted by a man who had walked up beside him.

"You might want to reconsider your flight choice."

Hawk turned to see a man about his age and height with auburn hair and brown eyes that reminded him of Cassie. "Excuse me?"

"I'm just saying going to Mexico would be a total waste of time when you should be going to New York."

Hawk had no idea who this man was or how he could possibly know his agenda. "And who exactly are you to be telling me where I should be going? How do you even know where I am going?"

"The name is Trevor Marshall."

"Marshall?"

"As in Cassie Marshall's older brother...and FBI agent."

Hawk slowly nodded his head. "That would certainly explain the resemblance to Cassie. It doesn't, however, explain why you are here and what you are talking about."

Trevor stepped closer and held out his hand. "First of all, it's good to meet you. I've heard a lot about you."

Hawk shook Trevor's hand. "Can't say I can say the same about you. I knew Cassie had an older brother, but she didn't bother to mention he was with the FBI. So would you care to explain what you're talking about?"

Trevor sat in the seat beside Hawk. "I will. But let me give you a little background first. Cassie called me after the incident in the warehouse. She was, understandably, scared and upset. We talked for three hours. Then, Steven called and told me about what happened at the hospital and that Cassie was being moved to a safe house. I, naturally, got very concerned. She may be a very competent adult, but she's also my kid sister. How's your head, by the way?"

"It hurts like crazy, and I'm fairly certain I have a concussion."

"So you should be in a hospital right now. Why are you so determined to find Cassie? There are other agents who could follow up on the leads."

Hawk looked away from Trevor because he simply couldn't look into those eyes that were so much like Cassie's. "Because I promised her I would protect her, and I'm not going to break my promise."

Trevor had a feeling there was a lot more to it than simply fulfilling a promise. But whatever the reason, he knew this was a man he could trust. "Good enough. But seriously, you need to change your flight plan."

"Why's that?"

"Because the game has changed…and it's worse than we thought. The drive you and Cassie found had some encrypted files on it, which I know you're aware of. They sent it to our offices to get our tech expert to see if she could decipher it. And she did. That's when I got assigned to the case and headed straight here. But I was a little late, obviously."

"So what was on the files?"

"Turns out Espinoza is just a front man. We're looking at something much bigger than Enrique Espinoza."

"How much bigger?"

"Have you ever heard of Juan Torres?"

"Juan Torres? He's the biggest crime lord in New York. Are you saying he's the one behind all this?"

"The encrypted files were all about Torres's crime syndicate and his connection to Espinoza. Turns out Espinoza is simply a fall guy. He was meant to draw attention away from Torres and his syndicate. And until that flash drive, it was working."

Hawk was definitely not liking the direction of this situation. "So you think Cassie is in New York with Torres."

"You do the math. Was the attack on the highway something Espinoza would have done? Is there any reason for Espinoza to take Cassie? Would he have had the manpower to pull something like that off and have a chopper waiting?"

"No. I had already thought it wasn't his MO."

"Exactly. So don't you think you should turn in that ticket to Mexico and take this one to New York?"

Hawk looked at the ticket in Trevor's outstretched hand just as they gave the boarding call for his flight to Caracas.

"So how did you know I was here? And that I was going to Mexico?"

"I was on my way to my parents' ranch when I came up on the accident site. I started talking to Reed Duncan, and he told me all about you. He also gave me this." He reached in his pocket and pulled out Hawk's DEA ID badge. "We thought you might need it in New York."

Hawk shook his head in disbelief as he reached out and took his badge and the plane ticket from Trevor. "I guess we need to change gates if we're heading to New York."

Trevor shook Hawk's hand. "I think I'm going to like working with you, Hawk Logan."

"Same here, Trevor Marshall. Let's go find your sister."

Cassie opened her eyes and looked around, trying to focus on her surroundings. The pain in her head, however, was making that a difficult task. She gently touched her head and felt the stickiness and realized it must be dry blood. She found she was lying on a bed in a small bedroom. But it appeared to be a nice room, not some dump. She tried to push herself up from the bed and stifled the yell that quickly came to her lips. Apparently, the pain in her head wasn't the only problem. It appeared she might have a broken arm.

She lay back down long enough for the pain in her head and arm to ease some and then tried again. She sat up slowly and began to orient herself to her surroundings. She slowly stood up and waited to get her balance. Then she walked around the room. There was one window that was painted over so she couldn't see outside. It was also nailed shut so it wouldn't open. Other than the bed, there was no furniture in the room. Just off of the bedroom was a small half bath. Again, just essentials. There was a bar of soap, one small hand towel, and a roll of toilet paper. She checked the door, and as expected, it was locked from the outside.

She was being held somewhere, but where? And why?

How did I get here? Is it Espinoza? Where are Steven and Hawk? God, please give me peace. I am so scared right now."

She tried to recall how she got here, but she simply couldn't. She remembered Steven and the DEA agents getting them out of the cave and then driving down the highway toward St. Martin. Traffic had been stopped, and Hawk must have thought it was a trap because he told them to turn around and go the other direction. That's where the memories got sketchier. She recalled an explosion and feeling pain. And she vaguely remembered being carried and the sound of a helicopter.

Is that how I got here? Wherever "here" is. But why? None of this makes any sense. Are Hawk and Steven all right?

She was injured in the accident, so what happened to them?

Lord, please let them be okay. I really need them now. I need Hawk, Lord. I know it's crazy, but I'm in love with him. But I guess You already knew that. Please let him find me.

Cassie heard a key in the door and turned to see two armed men entering. They stepped aside and a very large, rather ominous man entered. Cassie thought he looked familiar but couldn't place a name.

"You have turned out to be much trouble. But that will not be the case much longer."

Cassie hesitated to talk but had to ask, "Why am I here?"

"To make a point. Don't get too comfortable. You will not be here long."

She heard the key turn in the door. She sat silently on the bed for several minutes; and then, slowly, the tears began to roll down her face. After some time, she pulled herself together, tore off some strips from the bedsheet, and went to the bathroom to clean and bandage her arm and head. She didn't know how, but she knew God would deliver her from this too.

Chapter 13

The plane landed at the airport at five o'clock in the morning. Trevor and Hawk grabbed their carry-on bags and walked out of the terminal.

"The bureau won't open for a couple of hours, so we should probably go grab us some breakfast."

Hawk just wanted to find Cassie, but he knew they needed to regroup and make a plan first. "Sounds good. Guess we need to get some food so maybe we will think a little more clearly."

"There's a great little diner just down the street from the office. We can try to form a plan while we eat."

"Sure." Hawk was distracted. All he wanted to do was find Cassie.

Forty minutes later, they were seated in a back booth drinking coffee and waiting for their food to arrive.

Hawk liked Trevor Marshall. He just wished they had been able to meet under better circumstances.

Hawk sipped his coffee as he watched Trevor. "I spoke to Reed Duncan earlier. He said Steven was out of surgery and doing fine. He's going to be in the hospital for a few days, however."

"That's good to know. Steven is like family. We all grew up together."

"Yeah, Cassie mentioned that. I know she and Steven have been friends for most of their lives."

Trevor smiled. "They were inseparable when they were in grade school. Always thought they would get together, but they just never liked each other that way. But they would do anything for each other."

Hawk sipped his coffee as he nodded his agreement. Just talking about Cassie made his heart ache. They had to find her. He didn't know when it happened, but at some point, he had fallen in love with Cassie.

The waitress brought their food, and they ate in silence for most of the meal.

Trevor finally broke the silence. "So what is the real reason you are helping me find Cassie."

"What do you mean? I told you I promised to keep her safe, and that's what I intend to do."

Trevor nodded his head, watching Hawk. "I get that, but I feel there's more to it. What exactly is your relationship with my sister?"

Hawk needed to answer carefully. "We don't really have a 'relationship.' I like Cassie." *A lot.* "She's gotten caught up in something she should never have gotten into, and I want to get her out, safe and sound."

Okay, obviously he wasn't going to get any more information. But he had a feeling there was a lot more to it than simply fulfilling a promise.

Trevor pulled out some money and tossed it on the table as he stood to leave. "Okay. Well, let's head over to the bureau and see if they can give us any new information."

Consuella Torres followed her husband into his office. She knew confronting him was as good as suicide, but she could no longer bear to turn a blind eye.

"What are you doing, Juan?"

With utter contempt, he turned and looked at his wife. At one time, he had loved her deeply. But the years of corruption and evil had turned him cold to everyone, including his wife and even his children.

"It is none of your concern!"

"You should let the woman go. She has done you no harm."

Torres raised his hand and struck his wife across her face. She swallowed a scream at the pain as she held her hand over her cheek and stepped away from her husband.

"You dare to tell me what to do? You have no right in my business. Get out of my sight while you still can. And do not go near the woman." He turned and walked to his desk, totally dismissing Consuella.

Consuella Torres knew her days were numbered. Her marriage had been a lie for years, and Juan was becoming bored with her as he had flings with much younger women. She would never be able to escape his reach, but she would not allow the young woman to suffer at the hands of her husband.

Trevor and Hawk walked into the director's office, hoping to hear good news.

"Marshall, come on in."

"Good morning, Director Richmond. Sir, this is Agent Hawk Logan with the DEA."

Hawk held out his hand to shake the director's hand. "Good to meet you, sir."

"Same here, Agent Logan. That's a pretty nasty cut on your head. Have you had it looked at?"

"No, sir. No time to."

"Hmm." Captain Richmond picked up his phone and punched in a number. "Stitch, meet me in the tac room and bring your sewing kit." He hung up and turned his attention back on the two agents.

"Sir, I appreciate it, but that's not necessary."

"Son, you're under my command for now, and I take care of my people. Stitch is our pathologist, but he can clean it up and sew it up enough that it won't get infected. You can get it properly tended to later."

Hawk was actually very grateful for the concern. "Thank you, sir."

"All right. Let's walk and talk."

The three men left the office and headed toward the tactical room.

"Warner and O'Bryan worked all night pulling up all of Torres's properties. It's quite an extensive list. He's quite the business man, illegal business man, but quite successful all the same."

They met with Warner and O'Bryan and found Torres had twenty-three businesses and other real-estate holdings. They talked while Stitch cleaned and sewed up Hawk's head.

Trevor asked, "So what now? That's a lot of ground to cover, and we don't have a lot of time and, I'm assuming, no warrants."

"We're working on the warrants. As for the ground to cover, I've got six teams that will be dividing up the properties and searching for Ms. Marshall. But until those warrants come through, we wait."

Hawk was growing very impatient and becoming very frustrated. "In all due respect, sir, I understand the need to follow protocol, but Ms. Marshall is being held hostage by one of the country's worst crime bosses. She doesn't have the luxury of time on her side. If we don't find her soon, it may be too late."

Trevor admired Hawk's tenacity. "He's right, sir. We need to find her. Fast."

Director Richmond understood their concern, but there was little he could do. "I know the urgency this presents, and I am also concerned about Ms. Marshall's safety. But if we go in without warrants, we not only risk lawsuits. We could put Ms. Marshall's life at even greater risk. As much as I want to put these teams into motion right now, we wait. This isn't just a rescue mission. This is our chance to finally bring Torres down. We've been trying to make something stick for years, but like the snake he is, he just keeps slithering away. We have a chance to charge him with assault, murder of two federal agents, and kidnapping."

Hawk was beginning to feel the anger rising. Was this man using Cassie's abduction as his opportunity to nail this creep? He started to speak, but Trevor put his hand on his shoulder. He knew what he was feeling. But he knew the director well, and he knew he was right.

"Sir, we understand, but there's got to be something we can do to move this along faster."

But before the Director could answer, one of the clerks interrupted them. "Sir, I apologize for interrupting, but this is urgent."

"All right. Excuse me, men. I'll be right back."

Director Richmond was only gone for a few minutes and had a completely different expression when he returned. "Men, we may have just gotten the break we were looking for. Consuella Torres is in my office. And she insists on speaking only to the agents working on the Cassandra Marshall case."

Chapter 14

Fear and anxiety were written all over the face of Consuella Torres. Trevor and Hawk were equally anxious, eager to know what she could possibly be here to tell them. Captain Richmond walked over to her and held out his hand in greeting.

"Hello, Mrs. Torres. I am Director Richmond. This is Agent Marshall with the FBI and Agent Logan with the DEA. Please have a seat."

All four sat down across from the Director's desk, tension filling the room.

"Now, Mrs. Torres, what brings you here today?"

She looked at the three men, still filled with anxiety. She knew, by walking into this office, she had officially signed her death warrant. As soon as her husband discovered her betrayal, her life would be over. But of course, she knew that, whether she had come here or not, her life was on a very short string. Hopefully, she could do something good before her life was ended.

"So you are the men who are searching for Cassandra Marshall?"

Director Richmond answered, "We are the main ones, yes. Do you have information on Ms. Marshall? Is that why you are here?"

"*Si*. I know where my husband is keeping her, and I want to help you save her."

Hawk asked, "Mrs. Torres, we certainly appreciate your help because we know it is imperative that we find her soon. However, you must understand our hesitation. Why are you doing this? Surely you are putting your own life at great risk by coming here."

"*Si*, I am. But my husband is going to kill me whether I come here or not. My hope is that I can do something good before he kills me. Please understand that the Juan you know is not the man I fell in love with and married more than twenty years ago. His heart has grown cold, and he is hungry for money and power. It was not that way in the beginning. I just can no longer watch as innocent people pay the price for his climb to power."

Trevor's heart went out to this woman. She believed she was facing death regardless of her choices today, but she said she wanted to help Cassie. He prayed they could trust her and she wasn't leading them into some type of trap.

"Mrs. Torres, we are sorry for what you are going through. We truly admire your courage in coming here today. So what information can you give us that will help us in rescuing Ms. Marshall?"

Consuela Torres reached into her purse and pulled out a piece of paper. She handed the paper to Trevor. He unfolded the paper and saw that it was a drawing of a floor plan.

She indicated a bedroom on the second floor of the estate. "This is where the woman is being kept. The door is always locked, so I will leave you a key outside the gate. Here"—she pointed to a point in the exterior wall—"there is a secret opening in the wall. You can go in here unnoticed and leave the same way." She showed them how to go up the back way on the estate to get to the room where Cassie was being held and where the guards would be located. "I will place a key under a rock by the hidden passage."

They all appreciated Consuela's help, but naturally, they were still somewhat skeptical of her motives.

Director Richmond offered, "Mrs. Torres, let us put you up in a safe house. We can protect you from your husband."

Consuela Torres shook her head. "There is nowhere safe for me. It is my understanding that Ms. Marshall was in a safe place. He found her, and he will find me. Please, get the young woman out. It is one last thing I can do." She stood and walked toward the door. "Your chances will be better if you wait until it is dark. But you need to hurry. I do not think he will let her live for long. He says he plans to make a point."

Trevor held out his hand. "Thank you for your help, Mrs. Torres. Your help is invaluable."

Mrs. Torres shook Trevor's hand and looked pleadingly into his eyes. "Please, just save the young woman." She turned and left the office.

The three men stood in silence for several minutes.

Richmond finally spoke, "So do you think she's reliable?"

Hawk answered, "It doesn't matter if she is or not. It's all we've got, so we have to take a chance this is actually where Cassie is being held."

"He's right," Trevor interjected. "It's all we've got, so we go with it. Besides, I think we can trust her. She was obviously a very terrified woman. She came here trying to do something right in the middle of something very wrong. So how do we work this?"

Two hours later, the plan was in place. Trevor and Hawk would go inside to extract Cassie. Richmond would have several agents surrounding the estate grounds, providing cover if necessary.

"All right, men, gear up. We move out in an hour."

As soon as all the teams were in place outside the estate, Trevor and Hawk made their way to the place Consuela had indicated by the wall. Hawk reached under the rock and found the key to the bedroom. Carefully, they made their way inside the wall and to the back door of the house. They cautiously made their way down the hall to the back staircase. As they neared the top, they heard men's voices and stopped, guns aimed and ready. After a few minutes, the voices faded, and they heard a door close at the far end of the hall. They glanced at each other, and Trevor nodded for Hawk to proceed.

The map Consuela gave them indicated that Cassie was being held in the third room on the left. They quickly made their way past the first two rooms and then stopped to listen. They heard no one else in the area, so they proceeded to the door where Cassie should be. Trevor covered while Hawk turned the key in the lock.

Cassie had no idea how long she had been in the room, but she knew it had been several hours, possibly more than a day or two. Her arm was in severe pain, but at this point, that was the least of her worries. She had wrapped her arm as tightly as she could with the strips of bedsheet she had torn off, hoping to help keep the bones as stable as possible and prevent further damage to the break. She ripped some more strips off the bedsheets and made a sling to keep her arm immobilized. Cassie was terrified. It was obvious his plan was to kill her although she had no idea why. She just kept praying for God's protection and peace.

"God, I'm really scared. I know You're here, and I know You're protecting me. But I can't help but be scared. And I'm scared for Hawk and Steven. Are they okay? Are they still alive?" Tears rolled down Cassie's face as she thought of Hawk and Steven. "I don't know what to do, Lord. I could really use some help right now."

Cassie jumped at the sound of a key turning in the door. Her heart was pounding with fear. Was Torres coming back to end this? She stood from the bed and backed up against the wall. The door opened, and Cassie's tears came for a different reason.

"Hawk!"

Hawk quickly wrapped Cassie in his arms and held her tightly as she wrapped her good arm around his neck. "You're okay, honey. We're going to get you out of here."

Trevor stepped into the room. "Yep, definitely more than just keeping a promise."

Cassie turned at the sound of her brother's voice. She flew into his arms. "Trevor!"

Trevor hugged her tightly as he kissed the top of her head. Pain was shooting through her arm, but at this point, that was a minor concern.

"Hey, kid. You are a beautiful sight. Now, let's get you out of here."

Hawk stepped up and placed his hand on her back. "Is your arm all right?"

"I'm pretty sure it's broken, but it will be fine. Let's just get out of here."

"Good plan. Stay behind Trevor, and I'm going to be on your back. Are you ready?"

"Past ready."

Hawk nodded at Trevor, and they carefully moved out and back toward the stairwell. They easily made their way back to the downstairs door and then began to cautiously retrace their steps back to the hidden exit. They were about forty yards from the opening in the wall when a bullet hit the wall just above Trevor's head.

He yelled at Hawk and Cassie, "Take cover!"

They had just passed a cinder-block storage building, so they quickly ran back and took cover behind the building. They had barely made cover when there was a sudden barrage of bullets.

Trevor spoke into his com, "Markham! We're taking fire! They have us pinned down behind the storage building, and we can't make it to the exit!"

Markham responded, "We're on it! Just hold your position until we give the all clear!"

Within seconds, it sounded as though an all-out battle had erupted. After about ten minutes, the gunfire began to slow down, and Hawk heard what appeared to be a helicopter. Carefully, he raised up to look over the wall. In the field just beyond the wall, he saw Juan Torres and some of his men boarding a waiting helicopter. He was going to get away.

Hawk lowered himself back behind the storage and turned to Trevor. "It's Torres! He's getting on a chopper!"

Trevor shook his head. "He's not getting away. We need to stop him. You in?"

"One hundred percent."

Trevor contacted Markham again. "Torres is trying to escape. We're going after him. Can you cover us to the opening?"

Markham responded, "Just say when. We've got you."

Trevor looked at Hawk. "You ready?"

"Almost." He turned to Cassie and handed her his handgun. "Stay hidden. Don't come out until we come back to get you. Understood?"

Cassie was fighting to hold back her tears. "I understand."

Hawk gently touched her face and then quickly kissed her before turning back to Trevor. "Now, I'm ready."

"We're really going to have to talk." He looked at his sister and told her, "Stay here, and stay safe."

Cassie looked at her brother. "Be careful."

He nodded his head and then spoke into his com, "Markham, you ready?"

"When you say."

"Okay, let's do this."

Hawk and Trevor made a run for the opening in the wall while Markham and his men covered them. They made it to the outside of the wall, and the chopper was already off the ground and would soon be out of sight—and out of range.

Without looking at him, Trevor yelled at Hawk, "Cover me!"

Not hesitating, Hawk began to return fire with the men on the helicopter as Trevor ran to the middle of the field. Trevor took his position and aimed his assault rifle at the helicopter. He pulled the trigger, and the chopper burst into flames. He and Hawk quickly ran to avoid the falling debris. As they watched, the helicopter, and all those on board, was destroyed. Juan Torres would no longer be a threat.

Within a few short minutes, the other agents began to arrive on scene.

Markham ran over to the wall where Trevor and Hawk were still standing, watching the debris continue to fall from the sky. "Marshall, are the two of you okay?"

"We're good. Torres was on the chopper. Is everything inside under control?"

"It's all secure."

"Did we have any casualties?"

"Fortunately, no. A few injuries, but nothing critical. A bit like the two of you."

Trevor looked confused. "What are you talking about?"

"I'm thinking both of you are going to need some stitches. Go get Ms. Marshall and get to the hospital. We've got this."

"Thanks, man. We'll catch up with you later." He turned to Hawk and saw the large gash on his head. "Guess that gash on your head is what Markham was talking about."

"Yeah, your arm's not much better."

For the first time, Trevor noticed the long cut on his arm.

He smiled. "Looks like Markham may have been right. Let's go get my sister and get to the hospital. Then you and I need to have a long talk."

Hawk smiled. "With pleasure. But I plan to talk to Cassie first."

As soon as they stepped through the opening, Cassie ran toward them. Trevor pulled his sister tightly into his embrace as she managed to say, "Thank God. You're alive. But your arm is hurt."

"I'm fine. You okay?"

Cassie nodded her head. She looked past Trevor and saw Hawk standing just behind him. Tears began to roll down her eyes as she ran into Hawk's open arms.

Hawk hugged her like he would never let her go. He finally stepped back and cupped her face in his hands. "You are a beautiful sight. I love you, Cassie. I was terrified I would never get a chance to tell you that. So I want to be sure you know."

Cassie smiled into his gorgeous steel-blue eyes as she softly answered, "I love you too, Hawk." She pulled his face down to hers and met his lips in a warm, tender kiss.

Trevor was still in disbelief at what he was seeing. But he didn't disapprove. Hawk Logan seemed like a good man, and he definitely seemed like someone who would love and protect his sister.

"Okay, you two. Let's get to the hospital."

Trevor required eighteen stitches in his arm, and Hawk received nine stitches on his head. Cassie's arm had been cleaned and x-rayed, and she was in an exam room waiting to get a cast. She had been completely exhausted, and as soon as they got her back to a bed, she had fallen asleep. Trevor had stepped out for a few minutes, letting Hawk stay with her.

She had been asleep for about forty-five minutes when she woke with a start.

Hawk was immediately at her side, stroking her hair. "It's okay, Cassie. We're in the hospital, and you're safe."

As soon as she began to orient herself, she started to calm down, and her breathing leveled off. "I had a dream. We were all blown up."

Hawk tenderly kissed her forehead. "I know, honey, but it was all a dream. We're all fine."

Cassie's eyes suddenly grew large. "Steven. I haven't had a chance to ask about him. You said everyone is fine. Does that mean Steven is okay?"

Before he could answer, the door opened, and Trevor walked in pushing Steven in a wheelchair.

"Someone asking about me?"

Cassie looked up to see Steven's wonderful smile and the cast on his leg. "Steven. Oh, you're a wonderful sight."

Trevor pushed him over to the bed where he pulled Cassie into a warm embrace.

"I can say the same thing about you." He sat back as Cassie settled back on the bed next to Hawk. "You gave us quite a scare, hon. I don't think I've prayed so much in my entire life."

Cassie smiled, "Me either."

Trevor interrupted, "Listen, I think you two have some catching up to do. Hawk, could I steal you for a few minutes?"

Hawk looked questioningly at Trevor but replied, "Sure." He tenderly kissed Cassie's lips and caressed her face. "I'll be back in a few minutes." He squeezed Steven's shoulder as he walked past him to go with Trevor.

Steven had a quizzical look on his face when he looked at Cassie. She knew she was going to have some explaining to do.

Chapter 15

Somehow, Hawk didn't think Trevor wanted to talk about the case. They walked across the hall to a vacant room, and Trevor closed the door behind him.

Hawk smiled. "Okay, so I'm thinking this has to do with your sister?"

Trevor didn't change his expression or his position. "I like you, Logan, but you need to understand. That's my baby sister in that room across the hall. I have protected her all my life. I guess old habits die hard."

"Nothing wrong with that. It's good to know she's so loved and protected. She's had you and Steven her entire life. Now, she can add me to the equation."

"I got that impression. I also got the impression that, somewhere along the way, Cassie regained her courage to touch a gun. Now, not that I'm upset by that. I'm actually glad she is finally putting the past behind her and getting back to the old Cassie. So my bet is that newfound courage has something to do with you."

"Possibly. She told me about Tad. I'm sorry to hear about what happened to him."

Trevor nodded his head in thanks.

"I knew she hadn't touched a weapon since the accident, but I needed to leave her alone to get the flash drive to Steven, and I wasn't going to leave her defenseless. So I convinced her to take the gun. And turns out, it's a good thing she did."

Trevor shook his head in confusion. "What do you mean?"

Hawk had assumed that Steven had told Trevor about the man in the house. But from the look on his face, he obviously didn't know.

"Do you know what happened at your parents' house?"

"I know that your position was compromised, and Espinoza's men, or Torres's men, broke into the house. Two men were shot and killed in the house, and you and Cassie managed to hide then escaped from the others."

"Yes, that's what happened, but did Steven give you any specifics?"

Trevor looked confused. "Specifics? No. I haven't really talked to him about what went down. What are you telling me?"

"Those men broke into the house before I got back."

The look on Trevor's face spoke volumes. It was the look of a protective older brother.

"Are you saying Cassie shot those men?"

"She shot one of them. I got back before the other man got that far and was able to take him out."

Trevor took a deep breath and leaned against the wall as he quietly asked, "Was she all right?"

"She was amazing. Of course, she was upset that she had killed a man, but she was so strong. I think that's the moment I realized just how much I loved her. I came close to losing her, and that scared the crap out of me."

Trevor continued to lean against the wall, nodding his head and looking at Hawk without speaking.

After a few minutes, he finally said, "So that leads me to my next question. What exactly are your intentions toward my sister?"

Hawk smiled. "My intentions? Well, my 'intention' is to love your sister unconditionally. Protect her with my life. And hopefully, walk hand in hand with her through all of our ups and downs."

"So this is serious?"

"Very. Do you have any doubts?"

A smile slowly crept across Trevor's face. "Nope. One look at my sister's eyes, and I knew she was hooked for good. Pretty much the same with you, and I don't even know you."

Hawk still wasn't sure where he stood with Cassie's brother. "Are you okay with it? Me and Cassie?"

"I'm more than okay with it. From what I've seen, Cassie couldn't have found a better man."

"I appreciate that, but I'm definitely the lucky one in this relationship." Hawk veered the conversation back to the situation at hand. "You know, we've never had a chance to talk about what happened out there tonight. That was some pretty sharp shooting at that chopper. What branch of service were you?"

Trevor didn't look surprised at the question. "Army Special Forces. Sniper unit."

Hawk nodded his head. "That would definitely explain the accuracy of that shot. I could never have made that shot, especially from that distance and in the dark. That was impressive."

"Comes from years of training and practice. So how about you? Which branch were you?"

"What makes you think I'm former military?"

"I don't know. Maybe the same thing that made you think I was."

Hawk smiled. "Marines. Two tours in Afghanistan."

Trevor nodded his head. "Thanks for having my back out there today. And for protecting my sister."

Trevor's phone rang, interrupting their conversation.

"It's Richmond." He answered the phone, and his expression became subtly serious. After a couple of minutes, he ended the call and looked at Hawk. "They found Consuela Torres's body in one of the upstairs bedrooms. She had been shot in the head at point-blank range."

Shaking his head, Hawk replied, "Man, such a waste. I was hoping somehow she had gotten away. I knew it was probably too much to hope for, but still…"

"Yeah, me too. Let's get back to Cassie."

Steven and Cassie were still talking, but both were beginning to look tired. Hawk walked over to the bed, gently kissed Cassie, and sat down on the bed beside her, carefully placing his arm around her. She leaned back into his arms, resting her head on his chest.

Steven watched the interchange between his two friends and smiled slightly. "So the two of you seem quite cozy. Did I miss something?"

Hawk tenderly kissed the top of Cassie's head as he smiled. "If you blinked, yeah, probably. I'm not even going to try to explain it." He looked at Cassie with such love in his eyes. "But at some point during all this craziness, I realized this beautiful woman was a part of me. And I can't imagine my life without her."

Cassie kissed his cheek. "That pretty much sums it up for me too. It was totally unexpected, but I'm not complaining."

Steven was shaking his head but with a smile still on his face. "Well, I guess it's just a God thing. Personally, I couldn't be happier. I think you two are a perfect fit."

Trevor had been listening and watching as they explained their relationship. "Well, if Steven gives his stamp of approval, that's good enough for me. Now, Steven, I need to get you back to your room before they send out a search party."

They all said their goodbyes, and Trevor left with Steven. Cassie got her cast on and was released to home. Instead of going back to her house, she wanted to go stay at the ranch. Hawk was concerned about her staying there after all that had taken place in the house, but she insisted on going there. She said being around the horses would be healing for her. Trevor and Hawk decided to stay with her for a few days until she was comfortable staying on her own again. It had been a harrowing few days, and Cassie was going to need some time to process everything that had taken place in such a short time. But the one thing she didn't need to process was her feelings for Hawk Logan. There was no question—she was totally and completely in love with the man.

Chapter 16

Cassie, Hawk, and Trevor stayed at the ranch for about a week. It was a time for healing and for growing friendships. Trevor had to return to Washington to report back to work. His and Cassie's parents were coming back in two days, so Cassie knew it was time to go home. But at the thought of going home, she suddenly realized she wasn't ready to be alone.

As she and Hawk were putting their bags in his truck, she turned toward him and decided to voice her concerns. "Hawk?"

Hawk placed the last bag in the truck. He turned and saw the look of concern in Cassie's eyes. "What is it, hon? Is everything okay?"

"Well, not really."

He gently placed his hand on her face as concern now crossed his face. "What's wrong? Is it your arm?"

"No, my arm's fine. It's just, well, I'm not sure I'm ready to stay by myself. I know it's stupid, but I still have some fear about Espinoza."

Hawk smiled tenderly at Cassie as he continued to caress her face. "It's not stupid to still have a sense of fear. Would you feel safer staying here with your parents? I'll stay until they get back."

Cassie was shaking her head. "No, my parents have no idea how bad this was, and I don't want them to know." She hesitated and then asked, "Do you think, I mean, if it's not a problem..."

Hawk completed her thought for her. "Why don't you come stay with me?"

A look of total relief came across Cassie's face.

"Are you sure?"

Hawk smiled lovingly as he cupped Cassie's face in his hands. He placed his lips on hers and kissed her deeply and passionately.

When he finally pulled back, the concern on Cassie's face had been replaced by a warm smile.

"I'm very sure."

Cassie warmly kissed Hawk. "I love you, Hawk Logan."

"I love you too, Cassie Marshall."

Cassie had been at Hawk's lakefront home for two weeks and was definitely beginning to feel less fearful. She knew it was time for her to go home, but she hated the thought of leaving Hawk. As they walked along the beach, Hawk sensed something was weighing heavily on Cassie.

"Penny for your thoughts."

Cassie smiled as she held Hawk's hand a little tighter. "I was just thinking about how blessed I am to have you in my life."

Hawk smiled as he tenderly kissed Cassie. "I think I'm the one who is blessed. But I get a feeling there's more going on in that beautiful head of yours."

Cassie laughed. "Oh, you do?"

Before Hawk could respond, his phone rang. He glanced at the caller ID before looking back at Cassie as he answered, "It's Steven. Hey, Steven. How you doing, man?"

"Hey, Hawk. I'm good. Sorry I haven't been in touch more, but it's been rather crazy since I got back to work. I'll be glad to get this cast off and get off desk duty."

"I know you will. So as good as it is to hear from you, I sense something's up."

"I sometimes forget the other reason you're called 'Hawk.' Those hawklike instincts still throw me. Is Cassie still with you?"

Hawk glanced at Cassie and got an instant feeling of dread in the pit of his stomach. He squeezed her hand a little tighter as he answered, "Yes, we're on the beach. What's going on, Steven?"

There was a slight hesitation on Steven's end of the phone. "Trevor's flying in. He'll be here in about an hour. We'll be at your house as soon as he comes by here and picks me up."

"Trevor? Steven, this sounds serious. Is there something we need to know?" He saw the concern on Cassie's face at the mention of Trevor's name.

"I really don't know. He just said it was urgent and he was on his way here. We'll be there in a couple of hours."

"Okay. See you in a couple of hours." Hawk put the phone back in his pocket.

Cassie saw the look on Hawk's face and knew something wasn't right. "Hawk? What's wrong? Has something happened to Trevor?"

Hawk didn't really know what to tell her. He pulled her into his arms. "Trevor's fine. And honestly, I don't know what's wrong, but he and Steven will be here in a couple of hours."

"Trevor's coming here? Does this have something to do with Torres and Espinoza?"

"I don't know. But if it does, we'll deal with it." He pulled her close as he kissed the side of her head.

As they slowly walked back to the house, Hawk prayed this wasn't as serious as he feared.

Trevor and Steven arrived at Hawk's house about two hours later. It was a gorgeous day, so they all went outside to the deck. Hawk and Cassie sat together on the glider while Trevor and Steven took chairs across from them.

Hawk wasted no time. As Cassie clung to his hand, he asked, "So what's going on guys? Trevor, I don't think you would hop a plane if it wasn't serious."

"Yeah, I guess that was a pretty big clue. I know you're all concerned, so I won't drag this out. The man on the helicopter wasn't Juan Torres."

There was stunned silence as the three of them tried to absorb what Trevor was saying.

Steven was the first to respond. "What do you mean? You and Hawk both saw him get on the helicopter."

Trevor nodded his head. "Yes, we did. At least we thought we did."

Hawk wasn't liking where this was going. "But it looked just like Torres, and even though the DNA match wasn't 100 percent conclusive, it was at least a partial match. If it wasn't him, then who was it?"

"It was his brother, Eduardo."

Steven said, "So he was a decoy. Torres knew the two of them were built enough alike that, in the dark, we wouldn't be able to tell the difference. And if there was a problem and the only way to identify the body was with DNA, the results would be close enough to fool us. But the agents searched the house, and there was no sign of him. Where did Juan Torres go?"

"They discovered a tunnel under the estate that comes out on Martinique Avenue. Our assumption is, while all the gunfire was taking place, Torres and some of his men made their escape through the tunnel."

Hawk felt Cassie's body tense as she held his hand a little tighter.

She managed to ask, "Trevor, what does all this mean?"

Trevor heard the fear in his sister's voice and hated that this nightmare might not be over for her—or any of them.

"It means we're still in danger until Torres and Espinoza are located. It's possible Torres will just let it go and move on with his business, but I'm not betting on that happening. Torres is a cold man. He killed his wife, and"—he hesitated as he looked at Cassie— "he would have done the same to you if Hawk and I hadn't gotten there when we did."

Hawk knew fully the implications of what Trevor was saying. "So Cassie is still at risk."

"Yes, unfortunately, she might be. But you and I could be also. We're the ones responsible for blowing his cartel apart. I know you're not going to like what I have to say…"

Hawk knew what was coming and finished Trevor's thought. "Cassie has to go into hiding again."

"I'm afraid so. We have agents working the case, and they have some strong leads on Espinoza which, hopefully, will lead us to Torres."

Steven spoke up, "Okay, I get that Cassie needs to hide, but she can't do it alone. And where is she possibly going to go that Torres won't find her?"

"I've been thinking about that ever since I got word of all this." He looked at Hawk and Cassie. "One of our agents has a cabin in the

Blue Ridge Mountains. It's fairly secluded and far enough from here that it might be harder for Torres to locate you."

"So you're hoping to buy us some time."

"Basically, yes."

Cassie asked, "So I'm going to a cabin somewhere in the mountains of North Carolina until you catch Torres...or he finds me, whichever comes first. But who's going to go with me?

Without hesitation, Hawk spoke, "I am."

Everyone looked at him.

"If you think I'm going to allow some agent who doesn't even know Cassie be responsible for her safety, you're crazy. Either I go, or she doesn't."

A smile slowly crossed Steven's face as he looked at Trevor. "That was your plan all along, wasn't it?"

Trevor smiled. "Well, it was my hope." He looked at Hawk. "I know no one will keep her safer than you. If I have to place my sister's life in anyone's hands, I want it to be yours."

Hawk nodded his head slowly, grateful for the show of confidence from Cassie's brother. "So when do we leave?"

Trevor hesitated before answering. "Within the hour."

Cassie had held it together for as long as she could. The tears now began to slowly roll down her face as she softly replied, "So soon?"

Hawk pulled her close as he held her tightly in his arms. "We're going to be fine, hon. We'll get through this."

Cassie clung to him as she cried, "I know. But how much longer? When is this going to end?"

Steven put his hand on her back as he gently rubbed in a calming motion. "We're going to find them, Cas. But until we do, Hawk is going to keep you safe. Trevor and I are going to be in the loop too. None of us are going to let anything happen to you."

Cassie wiped her tears as she looked at Steven. "You know you can't promise that. Juan Torres is a dangerous man. If he wants any of us dead, he's not going to stop until we are."

Trevor spoke up, "Then we'll just have to find him first. Trust us, Cas."

Cassie wrapped her arms around her brother's neck as he pulled her into a tight embrace. "I totally trust you. All of you. I love you, Trevor."

With emotion in his voice, he answered, "I love you too."

After a few minutes, Hawk stood up. "Well, I guess, if we're going to the Blue Ridge Mountains, we need to get packed and on the road."

Cassie stepped away from her brother and put her hand in Hawk's. "I guess we better." She looked at Steven and Trevor with a new look of determination and strength. "We'll be right back."

They walked upstairs together to pack their bags and get ready to go into hiding once again.

Chapter 17

It had been a long three-hour drive to the Blue Ridge Mountains, but they were finally turning onto the road that led to the cabin. Hawk and Cassie had been talking for most of the drive, but for the last half hour, Cassie had been noticeably quiet. Hawk reached across the seat and took her hand in his and squeezed it comfortingly. She held tightly to his hand as she smiled at him in silence.

Ten minutes later, they pulled up in front of the cabin.

"Well, this looks like our new home away from home."

Cassie smiled tentatively. "I guess so."

He gently touched her cheek. "We're going to be okay, Cassie."

"I want to believe that, but I'm scared."

"I'm scared too, but we'll get through this together. We're not going to let Torres win this time. Trevor said they're closing in on Espinoza which means they're getting closer to Torres."

Cassie sighed deeply but had no reply.

"Let's get our things and get inside."

Cassie was afraid the cabin was going to be a rustic, run-down hunting cabin, but she was pleasantly surprised to find she was wrong. It was actually quite nice. There was a large living room with a big-screen TV, a fairly large kitchen with an eat-at island, a dining room with a table and six chairs, two large bedrooms with an attached bathroom, and a large deck at the back complete with a hot tub and large grill.

"Well, I'll have to say I'm quite surprised."

Hawk smiled. "You were expecting a dump."

She laughed at his assessment. "You already know me so well."

He tenderly kissed her. "Yes, I do, and I love everything about you. Now, how about you take the bedroom on the left, and I'll get the other one."

"Sounds good to me. I think I'll go unpack while you check in with Trevor."

Hawk put his bags down in the bedroom across from Cassie's room and stepped out onto the deck to call Trevor. He answered immediately.

"I assume you must be anxious. You answered before it even had time to ring."

Trevor smiled to himself. "Yeah, I guess I'm a little anxious. So did you make it there all right?"

"We did. Everything looks good so far. I'm going to check things out as soon as I get off here and find some spots to stash some weapons…just in case."

The thought of that made Trevor nervous, but he was thankful that Hawk was forward thinking enough to do that.

"I think that's a good idea. Hopefully, you won't need to use them, but it's good to be prepared. So how's Cas holding up?"

"On the surface, she's strong as ever. But I know how scared she is. Man, she's a journalist. This isn't something she's used to dealing with. None of this was even her fault. She had no clue about Torres's involvement in this, but now she's being hunted. It's just not right."

"I know. But I want to tell you something. My sister has always been a strong person. That's just how she's built. When Tad died, though, a piece of Cassie died too. These last few weeks, I've seen the old Cassie again. That's on you, Hawk. You've allowed her to feel safe and secure again, and that's renewed her spirit. She'll get through this because of you. Thank you for taking care of my sister."

"Truth be told, she's the one who saved me. I didn't realize just how lost I was until I met her. Trevor, I don't know what the future holds, but I'll die before I let anything happen to Cassie."

"Let's just keep praying that God keeps that hedge of protection around both of you. He's going to get all of us through this and help us end the tyranny that is Juan Torres."

"I pray you're right. I hear Cassie in the kitchen, so I'm going to go check on her. We'll check in again tomorrow."

"Godspeed, Hawk."

"Thanks, Trevor."

Hawk stood on the deck for a few minutes, taking in the scenery and enjoying the peace and solitude of the beautiful Blue Ridge Mountains.

Lord, I don't know what's going to happen over the next few days or weeks, but I know You've got this. Keep me focused and guide me to know what to do to get Cassie safely out of this. I can't do this without you, Lord. I trust You completely.

He took a deep breath and then went to the kitchen to join Cassie. Yes, the future might be uncertain; but no matter what, he knew God was in control.

The last five days had gone by without incident. On the second day at the cabin, Hawk and Cassie had gone into the mountains and located three secluded spots and hidden some assault rifles, handguns, and ammunition. Hopefully, they would not be needed, but Hawk had learned to always be prepared for any situation.

They had spoken to Trevor and Steven at least once every day. That contact had been their only connection to the outside world. As they sat on the back deck of the cabin watching the early morning sunrise, Hawk reached over and took Cassie's hand in his.

"Are you okay?"

Cassie smiled as she linked her fingers with his. "I guess that depends on your definition of 'okay.'"

Hawk laughed. "That's true. I know this is hard for you, but hopefully, it won't be much longer until we can go home."

"I'm just glad I'm here with you. I don't think I could have faced all of this without you."

Hawk cupped her face in his hand as he leaned in and placed his lips on hers. He kissed her with a warmth and passion that she had never known before. When he finally pulled away, they were both breathless.

As he caressed her face, he got lost in her luscious eyes. "I love you, Cassie. God may have brought us together under some rather unique circumstances, but I will be forever grateful that He brought us together."

"So will I."

Hawk's phone rang, interrupting their quiet moment.

He gave her a quick kiss before answering a call from Trevor. "Hey, Trevor. I wasn't expecting to hear from you so early."

"I wasn't expecting to call so early."

Hawk heard the hesitation in Trevor's voice and knew something was up. "Is there a problem?"

"Yes, and no. Is Cassie with you?"

"She's right here. I have you on speaker."

Cassie spoke to her brother, "Trevor, has something happened?"

"Hey, Sis. You holding up all right?"

"As well as can be expected. Trevor, what's going on?"

"Espinoza's body was fished out of the Hudson Bay last night."

Hawk ran his hand through his hair in frustration. "What happened?"

"He had a bullet through his head. Looked like an execution. We're guessing Torres is tying up loose ends. Espinoza's position in the organization had been compromised, so Torres didn't need him any longer."

Hawk sighed as he held tightly to Cassie's hand. "Okay, I probably know the answer to my next question, but here goes anyway. You said yes and no. There was a problem. Espinoza being dead isn't really a problem, so what's the problem?"

"Espinoza was connected to Cassie, so now that he's out of the picture, we're afraid he's going to focus on Cassie. Chances are he's returning to Mexico since his cartel is pretty much done in New York. He won't want to leave any loose ends."

"And Cassie is a loose end."

"I'm afraid so. I know you've taken every possible precaution, but be sure you're watching everything. You still have my emergency code in your phone, don't you?"

"I do."

"Just remember that my team and I can be there in less than an hour if you need us."

"I know. Thanks, Trevor."

"I'm praying for you guys. Cas, I love you, hon."

With emotion in her voice, she answered softly, "I love you too, Trev."

Hawk put his phone back in his pocket as he pulled Cassie to her feet. "Let's go for a walk."

"I'd like that. I'll go grab my jacket."

Forty minutes later, they were sitting on the banks of the James River, soaking in the sun and fresh mountain air. The gentle sound of the river and the sweet chirping of the birds helped to calm some of the anxieties. Cassie sat close to Hawk, resting her head on his shoulder as he held her securely in his arms.

"This is so beautiful. It's just so sad why we're here. Someday I want to come back with you when we can just enjoy God's beautiful creation without looking over our shoulder constantly."

Hawk tenderly kissed the side of her head. "That's a promise." Hawk turned to face Cassie and simply had to speak his heart. "Cassie, it sometimes scares me how much I love you. I have a hard time remembering what my life was like before you. Even more, I can't imagine my life without you. I know this is probably bad timing, and I don't have a ring. But, Cassie, I want to spend the rest of my life with you. When we get out of this crazy mess, I want to marry you. I don't want to walk through this life without you."

Cassie looked at Hawk with tears in her eyes. "Hawk, are you seriously asking me to marry you?"

Softly he answered, "I seriously am. So what do you say?"

She gently touched his face as tears now rolled down her cheeks, and she quietly replied with a smile on her face, "I say yes. Yes, yes, yes! I love you, Hawk, and I can't imagine my life without you either. Nothing would make me happier than to be your wife."

With a conflicted smile, he tenderly, deeply kissed her. They both knew the danger they still faced, but now they had even more to fight for. As the kiss lingered and deepened, they knew that this was right and, somehow, they were going to survive.

Chapter 18

It had been two weeks since the body of Enrique Espinoza had been discovered floating in the Hudson Bay, and there was still no sign of Juan Torres. Cassie and Hawk went for walks almost every day. Even though Cassie loved the time with Hawk, she knew the walks were more than just an opportunity to spend time together. Hawk never said anything, but Cassie knew. He was using the time to scope out possible escape routes should their location be compromised. He also would check on the weapons he had hidden. They both hoped they would never need either, but it was reassuring to know they had some options.

Cassie woke to the smell of bacon and biscuits. She quickly showered and dressed and then joined Hawk in the kitchen. She walked up behind him as he set the biscuits out of the oven and wrapped her arms around his waist as she laid her head on his back.

"Thank you for cooking breakfast. It smells wonderful."

Hawk smiled as he put his hands over hers. "You're welcome." He turned around and pulled her close to him as he wrapped her in his arms. "You are a beautiful sight to see first thing in the morning."

Cassie smiled as she warmly kissed him. "So are you. I'm starved. Do you think we can eat?"

Hawk smiled as he tenderly kissed her. "Yes, ma'am, I think we can. How about you pour us some coffee, and I'll get the food on the table. I assume you want some honey for your biscuits?"

"Of course I do." She winked as she turned to pour a couple cups of coffee.

Thirty minutes later, they were both sufficiently full.

"So you up for a walk? It's a beautiful morning, and I thought maybe we could go up the south side of the mountain. The view down to the river is pretty awesome."

"Hawk, you know I am well aware of the real reason we go on these walks, aren't you?"

Hawk tried to appear clueless to her meaning. "What do you mean?"

"Come on, babe. Yes, going for frequent walks is refreshing. It's a wonderful time for us to be together, and it's a great way to get out of this cabin. But we both know the main reason we go for those walks. Even if I wasn't a journalist, I could have figured it out."

She knew he was checking on the weapons he had stashed away in the mountains and checking the surroundings for any new intruders to the area.

He shook his head as he smiled. "Yes, I knew you were aware of my ulterior motive. You were just too nice to say anything."

"Well, nice may not be the reason. If I didn't say anything, it didn't seem so real."

Hawk wiped his hands on the dishcloth and pulled Cassie into his arms. He held her tightly and kissed the side of her head. "Baby, I know this is hard. I'm so sorry you're having to go through all this."

With her head snuggly against his chest, she cherished his warmth and strength as she wrapped her arms around him and held him close. "I'm sorry you got pulled into it. It's just so surreal. I mean, all this started because of Carson and that stupid flash drive. Don't misunderstand me. I'm glad we found the drive and got all the information from it. I just don't understand why Torres is still after me. I can't do anything to him."

Hawk stepped back and tenderly caressed Cassie's face, never taking his gaze from her soft brown eyes. "It's not what you can do to him that has Juan Torres so angry. It's what he thinks you have already done. We both know that Carson was responsible for everything and you had nothing to do with actually stealing the information, but Torres doesn't know that. And even if he did know, I don't think he would really care. Now, we're not going to dwell on this.

God has been with us through all of this. He's not going to leave us now. Do you trust that?"

Cassie slowly nodded her head. "Yes. I trust that."

Hawk met her lips in a kiss that left her knees weak. With a warm smile, he asked, "Now, are you ready for that walk?"

She took a deep breath as she smiled at him. "I'm not sure I can."

Hawk laughed as he kissed her again and sat her down on a chair. "Why don't you sit here and get your walking legs back while I clean up. Then we'll go for that walk."

"That might be a good idea."

After about an hour and a half hike up the mountain, Cassie and Hawk began to make their way back to the cabin.

"I know it's only been a short time since breakfast, but that hike has worked up an appetite. What do you think we can have for lunch?"

Hawk laughed at her question. "You're just using the hike as an excuse. I don't know how you can possibly eat like you do and stay so small."

"Fast metabolism."

He just smiled and shook his head. "I was thinking pizza sounded pretty good. Would that curb your appetite?"

"I think it would."

They were within several yards of the cabin when Hawk suddenly grabbed Cassie's arm and pulled her down beside him behind some trees and underbrush. She started to ask what was going on, but Hawk put his finger on his lips to tell her to be quiet. Then he nodded toward the cabin. Cassie raised up enough to see the cabin, and what she saw made her heart sink. There were two armed men standing outside the back door of the cabin, two outside the front door of the cabin and one beside the truck. Juan Torres had found them.

Chapter 19

Trevor was sitting at his desk when he felt his phone vibrate. He looked at the number and felt the adrenaline begin to pump. Hawk had called in the emergency code. Torres had found them. He instantly contacted his team of seven agents and told them to be at the airfield in fifteen minutes, wheels in the air in twenty. They were headed to North Carolina and the Blue Ridge Mountains. He just prayed they wouldn't be too late.

Anxiety in her voice, Cassie whispered, "Hawk, what do we do?"

"We're going to run up the mountain. But first, stay down."

Before she could question him, there was a loud explosion, and Hawk was on top of her, shielding her from any possible flying debris.

After a few seconds, he glanced toward the cabin and then pulled Cassie to her feet. "Let's go!"

Cassie looked at the cabin, or what was left of it. The explosion had apparently been the cabin blowing up. There was no sign of the armed men, but even if the explosion had taken them out, she knew there were probably more somewhere—and they would be right behind them.

As they ran up the mountain, Cassie asked, "What just happened?"

"There were two codes that Trevor gave me. One code was to alert him that we were safe in the cabin and needed backup."

"And the other code?"

"The other code was a dual code. It alerted Trevor that we needed help and were unable to return to the cabin." He hesitated before continuing.

"And the explosion? What was that?"

"The code also triggered an alarm that set off the explosives, hopefully taking out most, if not all, of the armed men and, if we're lucky, making any others looking for us think we were inside that cabin when it blew up."

Cassie grabbed his arm and stopped him as he turned to face her. "There were explosives set in the cabin the entire time?"

"Cassie, I'm sorry I didn't tell you. But I was hoping we wouldn't need to detonate them and you would never need to know. I know you are an amazingly strong woman, which is one of your many traits that I find attractive. But, babe, there's so much going on. It was just one less thing for you to worry about."

"It's okay. I know you meant well."

He kissed her quickly and then took her hand in his. "Let's keep moving. I can guarantee Torres and the rest of his men are already following us. We need to get to the guns that are hidden at the top of this ridge."

Hawk had his handgun with him, but he knew that wouldn't be nearly enough to protect them against Torres and his men.

Cassie nodded as she held tightly to Hawk's hand. They resumed their hike up the mountain, praying they would reach the top of the ridge before Torres's men reached them.

Trevor and his team were in the air and about thirty minutes from Hawk and Cassie. The airfield where they would be landing was about fifteen minutes from the cabin, or what used to be the cabin. Trevor knew from the code Hawk sent him that the cabin had been obliterated. It also meant that Hawk and Cassie were running for their lives. He lifted another silent prayer for their safety.

Hawk and Cassie were nearing the ridge where he had hidden the weapons when they heard the rustle of the leaves below them. They turned to see two armed men closing in on them quickly.

Hawk turned to Cassie with urgency in his voice. "Go! I'll hold them off while you get the guns."

"No! I'm not leaving you here. They'll kill you!"

"Cas, we're running out of time! All I have is my handgun. We need the rifles. Just go! I'll be right behind you."

Cassie didn't like the turn this was taking, but there was no time to argue. She had to trust that Hawk knew what he was doing. She quickly turned and hurried up toward the ridge and the hidden weapons. She had barely gone twenty yards when the first man reached Hawk. Hawk aimed his gun and shot three times. The third bullet hit the mark. But unfortunately, the other man had circled past him and was headed straight toward Cassie.

Cassie heard the footsteps behind her, but she just kept climbing. She had heard the gunshots and had turned to see one armed man fall. She realized the other man must have gotten by Hawk and that was whom she heard behind her now. She could tell he was getting closer, but she didn't dare turn around to see. But when she felt him grab her foot, she screamed. Within seconds, there was another gunshot, and the man let go of her foot as he fell dead from Hawk's bullet.

Cassie looked down the mountain toward Hawk, expecting to see him coming after her now that the two men were no longer a threat. But that's not what she saw.

Hawk had seen the man getting closer to Cassie and had taken aim, knowing that there was no way he could reach him before he got to Cassie. Just as he grabbed Cassie's foot, Hawk fired his gun. But that was all he remembered before everything went black. While he was focused on the man following Cassie, he had not heard Torres and his last remaining man come up behind him. When he turned to shoot, one of them had hit him over the head with a blunt object, probably the butt of a gun. He went down instantly.

Cassie watched in horror as Juan Torres hit Hawk with his gun. She saw Hawk fall, and her first instinct was to go to him. But she knew the only chance she and Hawk had of getting out of this alive was if she got to those guns and they were able to defend themselves. She stood for what seemed like minutes and then turned and ran toward the ridge.

Juan Torres saw her running away. He yelled at his man, "Get the girl! I'll take care of him!"

His armed man instantly took off after Cassie.

A couple of minutes later, Cassie reached the ridge where Hawk had hidden the guns. Quickly, she reached under the rocks and pulled out a handgun and ammo. Without hesitation, she loaded the gun. Behind her, she heard the click of a rifle and knew her time was up.

"There's nowhere else to go. Put your hands over your head and back away from the rock."

Cassie held the revolver in her hand, readied to shoot, and lifted a prayer as she quickly turned around. She had no time to aim; she just prayed the bullet hit its mark. And it did. She hit the man square in his chest. His rifle went off as he fell, but the bullet came nowhere near Cassie. She had no time to think about the fact that she had just killed a man—again. Hawk was in danger, and she had to do what she could to help. She quickly grabbed the rifles and ammo and ran back to where she had left Hawk.

When she reached the bottom of the ridge, she saw that Hawk was regaining consciousness. She also saw that Torres had his gun aimed directly at Hawk's head.

He kicked at Hawk, and she heard him say, "Get up! I do not wish to kill you while you sleep. I want you to see the bullet coming."

Hawk forced himself to sit up but still needed a few seconds to regain his composure. He was unaware that Cassie had returned and was watching their every move. She raised the rifle and took aim. But she didn't have a clear shot since Torres was standing behind Hawk. She stayed focused on him, waiting for him to move enough that she could try to hit him. When she saw him raise his gun and point it at Hawk, she knew it was now or never. Taking him out wasn't a possibility because of the angle, but maybe she could at least wound him enough to disable him.

Lord, help me. I haven't hunted in ten years. My aim from this distance may not be good.

She pulled the trigger.

The bullet hit Torres in the shoulder, and he fell backward, dropping the gun. Hawk was up instantly, but the blow to his head was making him unsteady on his feet. He managed to kick Torres's rifle away from him, but Torres came at him. However, the bullet wound to his shoulder was a huge deterrent. He was unable to fight

Hawk off and could not reach his gun. He realized he needed to retreat and regroup.

In frustration, Torres yelled, "We are not done!"

Then he turned and ran back toward the cabin, leaving Hawk standing alone. As soon as Cassie saw Torres running away, she rushed to Hawk's side.

"Hawk!"

Hawk had dropped to his knees by the time Cassie reached his side. He tried to stand up when he saw Cassie coming toward him, but the scuffle with Torres had knocked the wind out of him.

Cassie was quickly at Hawk's side. "You're bleeding. Sit still and let me bandage it."

Hawk winced in pain as he managed to stand to his feet. "We don't have time. Torres will be back, so we need to get out of here."

"If you don't let me get the bleeding stopped, you're not going to make it very far. It will only take a few minutes. Now sit still."

Hawk knew arguing was useless, and besides that, she was right. He was losing blood which was making him weaker. He needed it bandaged.

He slowly sat back down. "Okay, but how do you plan to bandage it, Doc?"

Cassie smiled as she ripped the sleeves off her white cotton shirt and tied them together to make a bandage large enough to wrap around Hawk's head. He was bleeding from the back of his head where Torres had hit him with the butt of the gun, but he was bleeding even more from a wound on his forehead. Apparently, he had hit his head on a rock when he had fallen to the ground from the blow to his head. She wiped the blood off as best as she could and then tied the makeshift bandage around Hawk's head. He probably needed stitches and most likely had a concussion, but this was the best they could do for now.

"Well done. Thanks, hon. Hey, wait, what happened to the man who came after you?"

Cassie took a deep breath. "Let's just say he won't be a problem."

Hawk saw the look on her face, and that was all the explanation he needed. He had to get Cassie out of this mess. "I'm sorry, babe. I'm not doing a very good job protecting you."

Cassie touched his face. "You took out the other man, but more importantly, you gave me the courage to protect myself. You've already saved my life."

"Would you please lean a little closer so I can kiss you?"

Cassie smiled as her lips met Hawk's in a warm, gentle kiss. She pulled back with tears in her eyes as she caught her breath. "I love you, Hawk. I can't lose you."

He tenderly caressed her face. "I love you too, and you're not going to lose me. We're going to get out of this. Now, we need to get moving. Torres will be back with reinforcements. The men we took out were just his first string. By now, he's probably already called in the second string. And I can guarantee there will be two to three times as many men the next time."

"So what are we going to do?"

"We're going to head back up the mountain and pray that Trevor and his team get here soon. We have enough ammunition to hold them off for a while, but not long if there are as many as I think there will be. But our best vantage point will be at the top of the ridge. From there, no one will be able to come up from behind. Are you ready?"

Cassie just nodded. She helped Hawk stand up, and they quickly began the climb to the top of the ridge.

While en route, Trevor had received intel that there was a flight coming into the airfield from Mexico. He had a strong feeling that the plane that was landing at the airstrip was loaded with Torres's men. He had contacted the local authorities and filled them in on the situation. He had also told them that under no circumstances was anyone to depart from that plane. The local sheriff had assured him they would secure the plane until Trevor and his team arrived. They were about ten minutes out.

As they landed, he saw the other plane on the airfield; and it was surrounded by deputies, local police, and a SWAT team. The sheriff had definitely secured the plane. Trevor's team quickly departed their plane and got an update from the sheriff. As they were talking, gun-fire erupted from the plane.

Trevor yelled, "Take cover! Take cover!"

All the authorities on the airfield ran for cover while returning fire. Torres's men had apparently decided they could fight their way out of this. The gun battle continued for over twenty minutes until, finally, the shooting from the plane fell silent.

"Hold your fire!"

A couple of police officers and a deputy had been wounded, and medical help was on the way. Now Trevor and his team, as well as the SWAT team, were cautiously making their way onto the plane. They pulled down the door and cautiously made their way up the steps. They had no idea what they would encounter. The gunfire had stopped, but that didn't mean that the shooters were incapacitated. Trevor carefully stepped around the corner and was instantly met with gunfire. They had their answer. At least some of the men were still armed and definitely not incapacitated.

He motioned to two of his men to cover him while two others made their way to the other side of the doorway. He indicated for the SWAT team to follow him into the aisle of the plane. He had been able to see at least three shooters. He looked to see everyone was ready and then gave the signal to go.

Trevor rushed around the corner, gun firing. His four men and the five members of the SWAT team were right behind him. They took cover behind seats as they returned fire. There appeared to be five shooters still engaging them. He had noticed four to five bodies in seats or in the aisle of the plane. No way to tell if they were all dead or if some were still alive. After ten minutes, it was all over. Trevor's team was fine as well as the SWAT team. Torres's men had all been taken out. They cautiously walked the aisle of the plane checking the bodies. There were twenty men in all, a virtual army for tracking down two people. Twelve of the men were dead; the remaining eight were still alive and would be taken into custody and treated at the local hospital. They had checked the cockpit, and the pilot and copilot had both been shot, apparently by Torres's men.

Trevor and his team left the processing of the scene to the local authorities and headed to the cabin. Hawk had managed to send him a text letting him know that all of Torres's men had been taken out, at least ten, but Torres escaped with only a wounded shoulder. So Trevor knew it was urgent that they find Torres. Thirty of his men had just been captured or killed. This, on top of everything else, was only going to increase his anger and push his feeling for revenge. Now more than ever, he needed to find Hawk and Cassie.

Juan Torres stood at the edge of the ridge overlooking the airfield, binoculars in hand, watching as his men were taken from the plane. Some were in handcuffs. Some were on stretchers, and the rest were in body bags. Fresh anger seethed within him. He put down the binoculars and watched from a distance as the anger continued to grow.

"They think they have won. But they have not. I will get the girl and the agent myself. This is all their fault, and they will pay." A cryptic smile crossed his face as he looked at a device he held in his hand. "Yes, they will pay, and I will have no problem finding them."

With one last look at the airfield, he turned and headed back up the mountain—an even stronger resolve for revenge now in his heart.

Chapter 20

Hawk and Cassie had been hiking for almost two hours when they suddenly hit a major roadblock. They came around a bend in the mountain where the only route was a narrow path around the side of the mountain. Unfortunately, there had apparently been a rockslide here, and the path was blocked.

Cassie was tired, stressed, and scared. She felt the hot tears stinging the back of her eyes. "Hawk, what do we do now? I don't think I can keep going. And you need to get your head wound checked. And..." She stopped, unable to go on.

Hawk pulled her into his arms and held her tight. "Cassie, I know you're scared. Truth be told, so am I. But by now, Trevor and his team have to be here. We just need to elude Torres and his men long enough to survive." Hawk felt his phone vibrate in his pocket. He looked and read a text from Trevor. "Well, looks like we just have to elude Torres."

"What do you mean?"

"Trevor just texted. Seems they were able to intercept Torres's second string of men at the airfield. Apparently, Torres is the only one tracking us. He has no men helping him."

"Just Torres? How's that possible?"

"The authorities detained his men on the plane until Trevor and his team arrived. Torres's men opened fire on them, and a gun battle ensued. When it was over, most of Torres's men were dead. The others were taken into custody."

"So you're telling me that Torres is coming after us alone? Why doesn't that make me feel much better?"

Hawk gave her a gentle smile. "Because he's a crazy, vengeful, heartless, extremely dangerous man?"

Cassie sighed. "Yeah, I think that's it. So what are we going to do?"

"We're going to find another way off this mountain." He scanned their surroundings and finally determined they should go back about a half mile and then head south, down the mountain.

"But won't that take us off the trails?"

"It's actually the best way to avoid Torres. He is most likely to take the trails, especially since he is by himself. So we stand a better chance of eluding him if we aren't on the trails."

Nodding her head slowly, she replied, "Okay. Then, let's do this."

Torres looked at the device he held in his hand and turned toward the path heading north up the mountain. He had gone about half a mile when he stopped. Instead of continuing on the path, however, he turned south and headed into the denseness of the woods. He had no clue where he was going, but thanks to the device in his hand, he knew he was going the right way. He was not far behind them. It would not be long now.

Trevor's team stood at the edge of the tree line, uncertain exactly which way they should go. Hawk had told him they had taken the path north from the cabin. The problem was there were two paths. They both went north, but one path veered left while the other veered to the right. He had tried to text Hawk again, but apparently, Hawk's phone had gone dead.

One of the agents asked, "So do we split up and take both paths?"

Trevor was shaking his head, trying to decide what to do. "No, splitting up is out of the question. We need to maintain a united force."

As he stood contemplating which path to take, a red-tailed hawk flew over and landed on the branch of a tree beside the path that went to the right. Trevor didn't know the story of Hawk's childhood experience, but for some unexplainable reason, he knew they should take the path where the hawk was. Without explanation, he started toward that path.

"We go this way."

His team didn't question his decision. They just followed.

It was getting late, and what little daylight they had would soon be gone. Hawk knew they needed to either get out of the woods or find somewhere to shelter. His preference was to get out, but it all depended on how well they could maneuver their way through the shadowy denseness. They were both exhausted, hungry, and thirsty. They had not planned on running for their lives, so Hawk hadn't packed a lot of supplies in their backpack. He stopped now and took off the backpack and sat down on a large rock.

Cassie looked at him. "Why are we stopping?"

He pulled out their last bottle of water and handed it to her. "We need to rest a minute and get some water. Sit here by me and drink some of this."

Cassie sat down on the rock and took the bottle from Hawk. She drank slowly, soaking in the refreshing wetness of the water. "Your turn." She handed the bottle to Hawk.

He turned it up and took a few sips, leaving a little more in the bottle for later. As he put the bottle back in his backpack, Cassie gently touched his bandaged head.

"Your head is bleeding again."

He placed his hand on hers. "I know, but it will be fine. I'm fine. I'll get it taken care of as soon as we get out of this mess." He saw the tears floating in her eyes and placed his hand tenderly on her face. "We're going to get through this. Do you trust me?"

"Yes."

"Do you trust God?"

"Of course I do."

"Then how can you go wrong? You've got God and me working to get us out of this."

She smiled a very tired smile. "Can't get much better than that."

He stood up and held out his hand. "So let's get off this mountain."

Cassie put her hand in his and stood up. But before they could move, a gunshot rang out as a bullet hit the tree beside the rock where they had been sitting. Hawk instinctively pulled Cassie down and behind a thicket of trees. He pointed his rifle in the direction of the gunshot, trying to see the shooter. He quickly scanned the trees at the top of the ridge, and there, forty yards above them, was Juan Torres.

Chapter 21

Trevor's team had reached the rockslide on the narrow path and knew they had to turn back. He thought he had made a mistake and taken the wrong path. There was no way Hawk and Cassie could have made it around that rockslide. In frustration, he turned his team around and headed back down the trail. When they reached the place where Hawk and Cassie had entered the woods, he heard the screech of a hawk and looked up. There in a tree was another red-tailed hawk. Again, with no way to explain it, he knew it was just a sign from God because he knew at that moment they had to go into the woods. This is the way Cassie and Hawk had gone.

One of his team asked, "Trevor, are you sure about this?"

"Positive."

"That's all we need."

Trevor and his team started into the woods.

"Stay down, Cas!"

"How did he possibly find us?"

"I don't know, but obviously he did."

Torres yelled down from the top of the ridge. "Time's up! You destroyed my business. You killed my men. You cost me everything! I must go back to Mexico and start again. I will not again be able to return to New York. And it is all your fault, Senorita Marshall. You should have stayed in your office and kept your nose out of my business. Now you and your agent friend will both die!"

Two more shots rang out.

Hawk returned the fire. He had no clear shot of Torres, and he knew he needed to get Cassie to better cover. The trees they were behind were barely good enough to shield one of them, much less two. And if Torres moved about three feet to the left, he would probably have a direct shot at them. Odds at the moment were in Torres's favor. He quickly scanned the surrounding area and saw a cluster of rocks about twenty yards to the right of them that would be a much safer cover.

"Cassie, listen to me. I need you to make a run for that group of rocks off to the right. Do you see them?"

"Yes. But I'm not leaving you."

"These trees aren't going to provide sufficient cover for us if Torres changes his position. I'll follow once you are safely behind them. I'll cover you while you get there. Will you do that?"

She nodded her head but didn't like the plan.

Hawk took his eyes off Torres long enough to glance at Cassie. "I love you. Now, go!"

Cassie ran toward the group of rocks, praying with every step. Almost instantly, gunfire erupted, and leaves and dirt flew up as bullets hit the ground at her feet. Just as she reached the rocks, Hawk heard her scream.

"Cassie!"

There was a slight hesitation before she answered, "I'm okay."

He heard her response, but he also heard the pain in her voice. She had been hurt. His first instinct was to run to her, but he realized Torres had shifted positions and there was no way he could reach Cassie without being a direct target. He knew Cassie had a gun with her and just prayed she didn't need to use it. But if she did, he also prayed she was able. He had no idea how seriously she was injured. But she was in a more secluded spot, so hopefully, better protected.

Trevor, where are you, man? We sure could use some help about now.

Trevor and his team had gone about a half mile into the woods with no sign of Hawk and Cassie or Juan Torres. But he knew they were going in the right direction. They had night goggles and lights if they needed them. For now, though, there was still enough light to see where they were going. Fortunately, there was a full moon providing sufficient light. But the deeper into the woods they went, the denser the trees became. The moon wasn't going to provide much light for long. Suddenly, they heard the distant sound of gunfire. It was coming from directly in front of them. Quickly but cautiously, the team moved forward toward the gunfire.

Please, Lord, don't let us be too late. Place a hedge of protection around Hawk and Cassie. Keep them safe from this maniac.

Hawk's head was pounding, and the blood from his head wound was running into his eye. But all he could think about was Cassie. He had called out to her again, but she didn't answer. The only comfort he had at the moment was knowing that, as long as he could hold Torres off and force him to maintain his position, Cassie was safe behind the rocks.

"God, I could really use some help."

The prayer had barely left his lips when he heard Trevor's voice from the top of the ridge.

"Torres! Toss your gun and come out in the open! You have nine guns aimed directly at you. There's no way out."

They all listened, but there was no response. It crossed their mind that, possibly, Torres had already been hit by the gunfire from Hawk. Trevor started to yell once more when, suddenly, Torres jumped into the open, aimed his assault rifle toward the ridge, and opened fire. Trevor and his team instantly returned fire. Torres was outmanned and outgunned. He was killed within seconds.

Trevor and his team ceased fire, and Trevor watched Torres for a few minutes, watching for any sign of life.

Finally, he yelled toward Hawk. "Hawk! Are you and Cassie all right?"

"I'm good, but I think Cassie's been hurt. She's behind the rock cluster. You check out Torres. I'll go check on Cassie."

"Go! We've got you covered. We'll be right behind you!"

Hawk was already running toward the cluster of rocks. His heart pounded when he saw the blood soaking Cassie's shirt. He knelt down beside her and carefully turned her toward him. She was breathing, but it was labored. He couldn't tell where she had been shot.

He gently stroked her hair. "Cassie? Honey, can you hear me?"

Slowly, Cassie opened her eyes and looked at Hawk. "Hawk? You're okay?"

"I'm fine, baby. Honey, I'm going to pull your shirt back and check out where you're hurt, all right?"

Weakly, she answered with tears in her eyes. "Okay."

He carefully began to pull her shirt back away from her camisole. He saw her wince with pain, and the tears roll down her face.

"Honey, I'm sorry. I don't want to hurt you."

"It's okay. How bad is it?"

Hawk looked at the bullet wound. There was so much blood it was difficult to actually see the wound. It was in her shoulder, but he couldn't tell for sure if it was through and through or if the bullet was still in there. He needed to stop the bleeding. The only thing he had was his shirt. As he was unbuttoning it to use as a bandage, Trevor came up behind him. He was instantly at his sister's side.

"Cassie, honey, we're going to take care of you." He looked at Hawk. "Wait. I have a couple of T-shirts in my pack."

He quickly pulled the shirts out, and together, they made a bandage and a sling for her arm. Once they had the bleeding under control, Trevor turned to Hawk and asked what they were all wondering, "So how do we get out of here? Do you know where you're going?"

Hawk shook his head. "No, not a clue. We hit a dead end on the path, so we circled back and headed this direction. I have no idea if we were headed in the right direction or not."

Trevor was concerned. "We need to get her out of here. Fast. She needs a hospital." He looked at Hawk's head and the blood-soaked bandage. "And from the looks of it, so do you. We have night goggles, so seeing won't be an issue. But if we don't know which way we're going..."

"I know. We could end up in a worse situation than we already are."

While they were talking, Cassie put her hand on Hawk's arm. "Hawk, look."

"What, hon?"

"Look." She raised her eyes toward a tree behind them. There on the branch was a red-tailed hawk. It appeared to be watching them. "That's the way out. It worked when you were twelve. It will work now."

Hawk smiled at her. Maybe she was right. It was certainly worth a try.

"Hawk, what's she talking about?"

"Long story. Short version is we're going to follow that red-tailed hawk out of here."

Trevor looked up at the hawk and chills ran down his spine. A hawk had led him to Cassie and Hawk, and now they were telling him this hawk was going to lead them out of the woods.

"You know, I should think you're crazy, but I don't. But when this is all over, I want the long version of the story."

"Deal. Now, let's get Cassie off this mountain."

Hawk stood to pull Cassie up but almost passed out.

Trevor grabbed him by the arm as he nodded to one of the agents. "This is Joe. He's going to help you down this mountain. We'll get Cassie. Just keep your eyes on that hawk since he's our ticket off this mountain."

The hawk didn't let them down. It was definitely leading them out of the woods. They had been walking for about forty-five minutes when Trevor yelled, "Hold up!"

Hawk turned to see Trevor and Agent Mendez laying Cassie on the ground. Adrenaline kicked in, and he was instantly at her side. "What's wrong?"

"She's not breathing!"

Hawk checked for a pulse, but there was none. He checked her airway to see if there was any blockage and then told Trevor, "You start compressions, and I'll do mouth to mouth."

They quickly began CPR. After a few tries, they had a pulse, and she was breathing steadily. Hawk laid his head on Cassie's forehead, totally spent.

Trevor reached over and put his hand on Hawk's shoulder. "We got her back, man. Now, let's get the two of you off this mountain and to the hospital." Trevor heard a bird in the tree above them and looked up. "Looks like our guide waited for us."

Hawk looked up at the tree. There on the branch was the red-tailed hawk. He had not abandoned them. God had not abandoned them. Hawk sighed deeply at the realization of what just happened.

He looked at Trevor. "Well, I guess we shouldn't keep our guide waiting. Let's get going."

Trevor picked Cassie up in his arms to carry her out of the woods. Mendez and Joe helped Hawk to his feet and supported him as they followed Trevor and their red-tailed hawk off the mountain.

An hour later, the hawk landed on a tree thirty feet from the highway—and twenty yards from Trevor's vehicle. They had pulled Juan Torres's body down the mountain but couldn't put him in the SUV, so two of the agents were going to remain with his body and wait for the sheriff and the coroner's unit to come pick them up. Trevor had already called it in and had notified the hospital that they were en route with an ETA of thirty minutes. He looked at his sister and became increasingly concerned. She was very pale and had still not regained consciousness since they had performed CPR on her. He knew she had lost a lot of blood and it was vitally important to get her to the hospital ASAP. He watched Hawk as he held Cassie in his arms. Trevor knew he needed stitches and had also lost a lot of blood. He also, most likely, had a concussion. But Hawk had no concern for his own welfare. He was totally focused on Cassie. Trevor drove as fast as he safely could. As he drove, he prayed God's continued watch care over Cassie and Hawk.

Chapter 22

As Trevor's SUV pulled onto the circle drive in front of the emergency room, Steven ran out to meet them. Trevor had called him as soon as Cassie and Hawk had gone on the run from Juan Torres. Steven had instantly boarded a plane to North Carolina. He had landed at the airfield shortly after Trevor and his team had headed into the woods in search of Cassie and Hawk. Once the call came in that they were on their way to the hospital, that's where he went. No one had said why they were going to the hospital, so he didn't know who was injured—or how severely.

Now, he rushed to open the door of the SUV. When he saw Cassie and Hawk, his heart sank. They were both covered in blood. Cassie was unconscious, and Hawk looked like he could pass out at any moment.

Trevor had opened the other door when he saw Steven. "Glad you're here, man. Help Hawk inside. I've got Cassie."

Steven didn't ask questions. He just helped Hawk out and supported him as they hurried into the ER behind Trevor as he carried Cassie inside.

Hospital personnel were instantly helping. They put Cassie on a stretcher and brought a wheelchair for Hawk and then pushed them into exam rooms. Trevor had gone with Cassie and told Steven to stay with Hawk. Cassie was examined quickly and had immediately been taken to surgery. The bullet wound was through and through, and she had lost a large amount of blood. When they took her up to surgery, Trevor went back down to the ER to check on Hawk.

Steven was leaning against the wall outside the exam room. When he saw Trevor get off the elevator, he straightened up and waited for him to join him. "How's Cas?"

"She's in surgery. She'll be fine. How's Hawk?"

"Lost a lot of blood and is getting stitches. Physically, he's going to be fine. But, Trevor, he blames himself for Cassie getting shot."

"What do you mean? It wasn't his fault."

"Maybe not. But that's not the way he's seeing it right now. I wasn't on that mountain. I didn't see where he and Cassie had taken cover. But I know he would never have done anything that would have put Cassie's life in danger. He would have died before he let anything happen to her. So exactly what did happen?"

"They were taking cover behind a line of trees. It wasn't a safe place to hide. Torres could have easily taken them both out. There was a cluster of rocks about twenty yards from them. Hawk knew Cassie would be safer behind those rocks, so he covered her while she ran to the rocks."

Steven sighed heavily. "And that's when Cassie got shot. That's why he blames himself. He thinks he sent her into the line of fire."

"But he didn't. If she had stayed where they were, Torres would have killed them both. He did the right thing."

Steven looked at Trevor. "Maybe you should tell him that."

"Maybe I should. Why don't you go on up to the surgery waiting area. I'll be up after I talk to Hawk."

Steven just nodded his head and walked to the elevator.

Trevor opened the door and walked into the exam room. "Hey, man. You look a little better than when we came in. Still look wiped out but not quite so beat up."

A very tired, weak smile crossed Hawk's face. "Well, glad I look better. I feel like I've been run over by an eighteen-wheeler. Is Cassie okay?"

"She's in surgery, but everything looks good. The bullet was through and through, and she lost a lot of blood. But they'll fix her up."

Hawk laid his head back against his pillow and closed his eyes. "Praise God."

Trevor pulled up the chair that was sitting beside the bed. "Are you up to talking?"

Hawk opened his eyes and looked at Trevor. "Sure. What's up?"

"I just wanted to thank you for what you did for my sister out there. You saved her life."

Hawk was slowly shaking his head. "I almost got her killed."

"You did no such thing. We both know, if you had stayed behind those trees, you would have both been killed. You saw a more secure area, and you got Cassie to it. You did exactly what I would have done. The same thing Steven would have done. Yes, she got shot, but she's alive and going to be fine. Her getting shot had nothing to do with your decision to send her to the rock coverage. This was in no way your fault."

"But if I hadn't sent her into the open—"

Trevor interrupted, "You would both be dead. I am very thankful that my sister was with you on that mountain. You need to realize you made the right choice. You did the right thing."

Hawk slowly shook his head. "I know. In my head, I know I did the right thing. But seeing her covered in blood…" He looked at Trevor. "This is the woman I love. I was supposed to protect her."

"You did protect her. And I have no doubt you will continue to protect her for many years to come. You need to understand something. Cassie is my kid sister. It has always been my job to protect her. Ever since Tad was killed, I've probably been a little too overprotective. I don't trust her life to just anybody. I have always trusted Steven but not really anyone else, even my brothers. You, however, are someone I totally trust to take care of my sister."

"Thanks for that, Trevor."

Trevor nodded his head and pushed back the chair as he stood up. "I meant every word. Now, get some rest. I understand you're going to be moved out to a room soon."

"Hey, about that. Do you think you could work some of your FBI magic and get Cassie and me in the same room? I just don't want to be away from her."

Trevor's mouth twisted into a slight smile. "I'll see what I can do." He gently tapped Hawk's shoulder. "Now, get some rest. I'm going to go check on Cassie, and I'll see you in a little while when they move you upstairs." Trevor left and headed upstairs to wait with Steven for Cassie to get out of surgery.

A short time later, Hawk was moved upstairs to a room. Once he was settled, Trevor and Steven went in to check on him. The nurse had told him she would be back shortly to start the blood. He was going to need at least a unit of blood to replace what he had lost.

Steven walked over and pulled up a chair beside the bed. "No offense, but you're still not looking so great."

Hawk gave him a weak smile. "No offense taken. I'm sure, if I look like I feel, I don't look very good. Maybe after getting that blood, I'll look better. Any word on Cassie?"

Trevor spoke, "She's out of surgery and will be in recovery for about an hour. Then they'll bring her in here."

"Is she all right?"

"She's great. Surgery went well. She got a couple of units of blood during surgery and is going to need at least one more once they get her in here."

A look of total relief crossed Hawk's face. He leaned his head back against the pillow, visibly relaxed.

After a few seconds, he asked, "Wait, you said they're bringing her in here? What did you do to make that happen?"

Trevor gave a slight laugh. "I just told them the truth. The two of you were involved in a federal case that is still under investigation, and it is imperative that I keep a close eye on both of you since your lives could still be in danger. Done deal."

Steven commented, "You said you told them the truth. Do you really think they are still in danger?"

"Probably not. But as Hawk is well aware, we don't always know all we need to know. At the moment, we are still investigating Juan Torres to see if anything else turns up."

"Do you expect something to turn up?"

Hawk answered, "For months, we have been after Espinoza. We had no idea he was actually working for Torres."

"He's right. We're almost certain Juan Torres is as high as this cartel went, but we want to be positive."

Hawk said, "Well, I don't care how you did it. I'm just glad Cassie and I will be in the same room."

The nurse came back in to get the blood started and put up a new IV bag. Once she was finished, Hawk quickly went to sleep. Steven and Trevor settled in to wait for Cassie.

When Hawk woke up about an hour later, Cassie was sleeping in the bed on the other side of the room. Trevor was asleep in the chair next to her bed.

"Hey, you feeling any better?"

Hawk turned his head to see Steven sitting next to his bed.

"Some. I think the pain meds have kicked in and that blood is bringing back some of my strength. How's Cassie? She looks so pale. Is she okay?"

"Yeah, doctor said she's going to be fine. They're giving her another unit of blood and possibly another one later. They're going to keep her for at least a couple of days. She's been asleep ever since they brought her in."

"Can you help me sit up?"

"Sure." Steven adjusted the bed so the head rose up higher. He helped Hawk scoot up in the bed and readjusted his blankets and pillows. "Can I get anything for you? Do you need something to drink?"

"No, I'm good—" He stopped what he was saying when he heard movement from Cassie's bed. "Help me get out of this bed."

"Hawk, you're not supposed to be up yet."

"Either you help me, or I'll get to Cassie on my own."

Steven knew Hawk well enough to know there was no arguing with him. So rather than have him fall, he helped him out of the bed and over to Cassie's bed.

Trevor had woken up when he heard Cassie beginning to stir and was standing on the other side of her bed. "Hawk, you okay?"

He sat down on the bed beside Cassie and took her hand in his. "I'm fine now." He gently stroked Cassie's hair as she began to open her eyes.

Steven had moved to stand at the foot of the bed. Cassie heard beeping sounds and muffled noises that seemed to be coming from a short distance. She slowly opened her eyes, trying to orient herself to her surroundings, and smiled weakly as she looked into the warmth of Hawk's eyes.

With emotion in his voice, Hawk softly said, "Hi."

"Hi." She looked around the room and saw Trevor beside her and Steven standing at the foot of her bed. "Am I in Kansas? Who's the Scarecrow? He was always my favorite. And I don't see Auntie Em."

Trevor laughed at her reference to *The Wizard of Oz* and felt an instant surge of relief at her humor. This was the Cassie he had always known and loved.

He leaned over and gently kissed his sister's forehead. "Welcome back. And I know you love us all, but my guess is Hawk would have to be Scarecrow. And Auntie Em switched out your IV a few minutes ago and will probably be back in a little while."

She laughed gently. "I love you, Trevor." She looked at Steven at the foot of the bed. "Hey, Stevie."

"Stevie? You haven't called me that since we were kids. Good to see those beautiful eyes again."

"Where am I? Are we back home?"

Steven smiled. "No. We're still in North Carolina. You just had surgery, and you're going to be fine. I had to come out here and keep an eye on these two."

Cassie reached up and gently touched Hawk's bandaged head. "No offense, but I'm not sure you did a very good job." With concern in her voice, she asked Hawk, "Are you all right?"

"I'm good. A few stitches and a little blood, and I'm good to go."

"I love you."

"I love you too." He wasn't sure he wanted to know the answer to his next question, but he had to ask, "Do you remember what happened?"

Cassie was quiet for a few seconds and then answered, "Yes. You saved my life."

Hot tears burned Hawk's eyes.

"Cassie…"

She squeezed his hand. "You sent me to a safer spot, and I got shot when a bullet ricocheted off the rock."

"What? You remember getting shot?"

"Yes. I had just dived behind the rocks when a bullet hit one of the rocks, and I felt the pain in my arm and the blood…"

Hawk touched her face. "Cassie, honey, I'm so sorry. I never should have risked your life like that."

She placed her hand on top of his. "If I hadn't thought you were doing the right thing, I would have refused to go. I knew we were easy targets where we were. If I had stayed, we would have both been killed. You saved my life by sending me to those rocks."

Hawk gently kissed her lips as a tear slipped from his eye.

Trevor had been silent during their exchange but now interjected, "See, she agrees with me, so I must have been right. I told you the exact same thing. Cassie is alive now because you made a very difficult decision at the exact right moment."

"Could I have a drink of water? I'm so thirsty."

Trevor poured some water into the cup on her bedside tray and positioned the straw so she could drink.

She took a few slow sips and then relaxed back against the pillows. "So how long do we have to stay here?"

Hawk replied, "They'll probably release me tomorrow, but you have a couple of more days. We'll be right here with you the entire time."

"Where's your room? Is it close to mine?"

Hawk smiled. "It is yours."

"What?"

Trevor spoke up, "I arranged for the two of you to share a room. I figured you couldn't have a better roommate. Besides, I'm thinking you may need to get used to spending a lot of time together."

Hawk smiled as he tenderly kissed Cassie. "We'll definitely be spending a lot of time together."

Cassie said, "Do you think we should tell them?"

"I don't know. I think we're both pretty spent. We might need to get some rest."

Steven and Trevor both said in unison, "What?"

Trevor said, "I agree you both need to rest, but you can't just leave us hanging. Seriously."

Steven had moved to stand beside Trevor, "So before you both get some rest, what is it you need to tell us?"

Hawk was holding Cassie's hand securely in his. "I asked Cassie to marry me."

She smiled at him and then looked at her brother and best friend. "And I said yes."

It took a few seconds for the news to sink in, and then Trevor bent over and kissed his sister's cheek. "That's wonderful, baby. You couldn't have picked a better man." He patted Hawk's shoulder. "And I couldn't have picked anyone better for my sister. Welcome to the family, man."

Steven interjected, "I second all Trevor just said." He bent over and kissed Cassie's cheek. "I'm really happy for you, Cas. But I'll warn you. You're going to have your hands full with this one."

Cassie smiled. "That's okay. I have a brother and a best friend who will help me keep him in line."

Hawk smiled. "Gee, thanks."

Trevor could see that Hawk and Cassie were both looking pretty wiped out and it was time for them to rest. "Okay, Dorothy, we need to get Scarecrow back to his bed and get you both settled down so you can get some rest. Otherwise, Auntie Em might not let the Lion and Tin Man come back."

Cassie gave them a very tired smile as Hawk gently kissed her and Steven helped him back to his bed. They were both asleep within minutes. The last few months had been stressful on them, and the battle on the mountain with Torres and his men took every last ounce of strength they had. They were going to need plenty of time to recoup, physically and mentally. Trevor and Steven stepped out of the room and let them sleep while they went to make arrangements for their return trip home in a few days. It was going to be good to get home.

Chapter 23

Hawk had only required the one unit of blood, but Cassie had received one more after the one she had postsurgery. She had quickly regained her strength but was still very weak and tired. Hawk had been released after twenty-four hours, but they had allowed him to stay in the room with Cassie until she was released. After four days in the hospital, they were all finally going home.

Trevor's team had flown back in the plane that had flown them to North Carolina; so the agency sent another plane to pick up Trevor, Steven, Cassie, and Hawk and return them home. Trevor and Steven were waiting in the circle drive with their rented SUV when the nurse rolled Cassie out in a wheelchair, Hawk at her side.

She smiled at the sight of her brother and friend. "It's good to finally be going home."

Trevor kissed his sister's cheek. "It's good to finally be taking you home." He opened the back door as the nurse pushed the wheelchair up to the SUV. "Your chariot awaits."

Hawk held out his hand to help her out of the wheelchair. "Let's go home."

"Music to my ears."

Twenty minutes later, they were boarding the agency plane at the airfield. Cassie and Hawk took the reclining seats at the rear of the plane while Trevor and Steven settled in to the seats in the middle. Within minutes of takeoff, Cassie and Hawk were both asleep, Cassie's hand securely tucked in Hawk's hand.

Steven glanced toward the back at his two friends and smiled, lifting another prayer of thanks. He knew how close he had come to losing both of them.

He turned back around and looked at Trevor who was also looking at the two at the rear of the plane. "So are you okay with them together?"

Trevor turned back around and smiled at Steven. He and Steven had been friends almost their entire lives. They were more like brothers than friends.

"I've never been more okay about anything in my life. I'll admit, when I first met Hawk, it wasn't a great impression. I thought he was a hothead who didn't follow rules and didn't care about how his actions impacted other people. But I couldn't have been more wrong."

"No, you couldn't. I've never known anyone more loyal and honorable than Hawk Logan. So what made you change your mind?"

Trevor glanced toward the two at the rear of the plane again. "She did. When I saw the way she looked at him and the way she trusted him, I started looking at him differently. And when I did that, I saw a very different person. He's the kind of person who would instantly lay his life on the line for someone he cared about. Like you said, he's loyal and honorable...and so much more. More importantly, he's a strong Christian. Can't lose when you've got God on your side."

Steven leaned his head back on the seat. "No, you can't."

Trevor watched his friend for a few seconds and then asked, "So how do you feel about them together?"

"Me? Couldn't be happier. But to be honest, I've known Hawk for years, and even though he is a good man, I would never have thought of putting him with Cassie. Guess it's a good thing God was in charge. I don't think you and I would have done a very good job as matchmakers."

Trevor laughed. "No, definitely not. But I'm really glad He brought Hawk Logan into our family."

"Me too."

An hour later, the plane was circling the airfield as it prepared to land. Cassie held Hawk's hand tightly, suddenly feeling anxious. She had been having bad dreams ever since the run in with Torres on the mountain, but she hadn't told anyone about them. Trevor had convinced her to stay on the ranch with their parents for a while, just until she felt a little more settled. She had agreed, but she was still nervous about being at the ranch alone. She knew her parents would be there. But they had no idea what she had been through, and she didn't want to burden them with the sordid details.

Hawk watched Cassie and knew something was stressing her. "Penny for your thoughts."

Cassie brought her thoughts back to the present as she turned to face Hawk. "Hmm?"

He gently touched her face as he pushed a strand of her hair behind her ear. "You look like you're a million miles away. What's bothering you?"

"Nothing's bothering me. I'm fine."

"Want to try that answer again?"

Cassie took a deep breath and sighed deeply as she put her head back against the seat. "I'm nervous about staying at the ranch alone."

"Honey, you won't be alone. Your parents will be there, and I'll be out there every day to visit."

She looked into Hawk's warm, comforting eyes and finally spoke what was on her heart, "I want you to come stay with me."

Hawk had a confused look on his face. "Why? I mean, other than just being able to bask in the luxury of my presence." He smiled that smile that melted her heart every time.

She laughed at him. "You nut." Then she got serious as she confessed to him, "I've been having dreams."

Hawk was instantly concerned. "Dreams?"

"They started in the hospital. We're on the mountain. Torres and his men are shooting at us. I get shot... You get shot... There's blood everywhere..."

Hawk pulled her close to him. "Honey, why didn't you say anything? There's nothing to be afraid of anymore. Torres is gone. Espinoza is gone. And Trevor said all the intel the agency has gathered confirms that Torres was head of the cartel. There's no one else to come after us. We're both safe." He kissed the side of her head.

"In my mind, I know that, but I can't tell my parents what happened on that mountain. Not all of it. I know I'm safe, but I just don't feel safe yet…unless I'm with you."

He turned her face toward him as he cupped her chin in his hand. "If you need me to stay with you for a while, I'll stay."

She smiled slightly as a tear rolled down her cheek. "Thank you."

Hawk's lips met hers in a warm, tender kiss. He would have loved to have kissed her longer and deeper, but with Trevor and Steven sitting a few rows up, he thought he should wait for a better time. "I love you, Cassie Marshall, and I can't wait to make you Cassie Logan."

"Neither can I." She returned his kiss as the plane began its descent to the airfield.

Hawk had stayed at the ranch with Cassie for two weeks. She stayed there for another week and then returned to her own house. Their physical injuries were almost healed, and their emotional injuries were well on their way. Cassie had worn her arm in a sling for those three weeks, but today it had finally come off.

She was spending the day with Hawk at his lakefront house, and Trevor and Steven were joining them for grilled burgers later in the day. As they walked on the beach with their fingers entwined, Cassie couldn't keep the smile off her face.

Hawk couldn't help but notice how happy Cassie looked. "You want to tell me what has that beautiful smile glued to your face?"

"I don't know. I guess several things."

"Like what?"

She kissed him deeply and passionately, which caught him by surprise. As she pulled back, he thought about how much he was looking forward to spending the rest of his life with her.

She looked warmly into his eyes as she softly replied, "Well, definitely, you for one."

"I like to hear that."

"And God. I stopped having those dreams shortly after coming home. That was because of you and God. You have given me so much love and a feeling of safety and security. And God has never left my side. Through all this mess, He's been there, holding me, protecting me—us—and reassuring me that He's not going anywhere. I just have such peace and contentment. And I owe all that to God…and you. I love you, Hawk. Thank you for loving me and protecting me."

"I always will."

They stopped walking, and Hawk reached into his pocket to pull out a small box. Cassie's eyes watered as she realized what he was doing. He dropped to one knee there in the sand in front of Cassie as he opened the box to reveal a stunning diamond-and-sapphire engagement ring.

"Cassie, I know you've already said you would be my wife, but I wanted to do it right…with a ring. I thank God every day that he brought us together and that He has protected us through everything. You are the person I never knew I was looking for, but now I can't imagine my life without you. I love you, Cassie Marshall, and I look forward to showing you just how much for the next fifty-plus years. Cassie, will you still marry me?"

Tears beginning to roll down her face, she softly answered, "Yes, I will definitely still marry you. I love you so much, Hawk."

Hawk stood up and placed the ring on Cassie's finger as tears of joy rolled down her face. He threaded his fingers through her long auburn hair as he pulled her face toward his and met her lips with his. Her lips parted as the passion and love grew and lingered in that kiss. She felt her knees growing weak and wrapped her arms tighter around his neck just so she wouldn't fall to the ground.

After a long, passionate kiss, Hawk pulled back, breathless and his heart pounding from love and desire. "It's going to be a great fifty-plus years"

Cassie smiled. "Yes, it is."

About the Author

Carol Oliver Turcotte lives in Kentucky with her husband and their fur babies. She has been a Kindergarten teacher for thirty years. In addition to writing, Carol enjoys cooking, sewing, and spending time with her husband, their family, and their friends.

CPSIA information can be obtained
at www.ICGtesting.com
Printed in the USA
LVHW020606010821
694125LV00004B/471